END OF THE TRAIL . . . .

A little spring ran out of the hillside near the bottom of the bowl-shaped meadow. Janet, Scott and Gene left the horses hobbled to drink and graze while they set up camp. The evening was peaceful. Mourning doves cooed into the evening while a family of killdeers scolded loudly at the invasion of their waterhole, making sharp noises and running along the edge of the spring. It was a pretty evening that was broken by a gruff voice that came down from the hillside above them.

They looked up. Three riders with their rifles ready to use.

"No fancy moves!" one of the men called. "Just stand up slow with your hands in the air . . ."

Spur Award Winning Westerns From Charter Books

THE HONYOCKER by Giles A. Lutz
THE LAST DAYS OF WOLF GARNETT by Clifton Adams
LAW MAN by Lee Leighton
MY BROTHER JOHN by Herbert Purdum
THE VALDEZ HORSES by Lee Hoffman

...and Other Exciting Westerns From Charter Books

BLOOD ON THE LAND by Frank Bonham
CHEYENNE DRUMS by Lewis B. Patten
GUN FEUD AT TIEDOWN/ROGUE'S RENDEZVOUS by Nelson Nye
LYNCHER'S MOON by Will C. Knott
RIDE THE HOT WIND by Lewis B. Patten

THE HORSE RANCH

Earl Murray

CHARTER BOOKS, NEW YORK

To my five young wranglers:

Lynette, Yvonne, Tina,
Ryan, and Pam

THE HORSE RANCH

A Charter Book / published by arrangement with
the author

PRINTING HISTORY
First Ace Charter printing / February 1983
Second printing / October 1985

ISBN: 0-441-34288-4

Charter Books are published by The Berkley Publishing Group,
200 Madison Avenue, New York, New York 10016.
PRINTED IN THE UNITED STATES OF AMERICA

Chapter 1

The sun was only a scarlet haze pouring from the east through the pines and into the grass meadows. Along the creek two horses with riders ran full speed through grass that was bright green from spring growth. Their legs stretched down to the bottom, hooves pounding the soft carpet of new grass, the riders bent low, riding without saddles to allow for greater speed. The haze turned to a ball of yellow light, firm in outline and intense in the spring sky. Up to now the horses had run neck and neck over the meadow, but at the last surge up to the lone cottonwood at the bend in the creek, the palamino stallion pulled away. At the end of the run, the young woman riding him laughed and turned to her younger brother.

"Scott, you'll never have a horse who can beat Clipper." She tossed her head, shaking her long red hair, and brushed it back into place with her hand. "Never."

"Don't be so cocky, Janet. Any horse can be beaten one time or another."

"Not today," said Janet, and galloped up the hill into the rising sun.

Scott sulked awhile, his twelve-year-old pride ruffled. Now he would have to be the one to go up to the C Bar S and lead a pair of brood mares back while Janet went to town for supplies. She always got the good jobs. Maybe it had been his fault, though. It had been his turn to go to town, but Janet had talked him into a bet he knew he couldn't win. Yet he couldn't resist a horse race. And now he'd pay for it by spending his day with two plug horses instead of on the streets of Forsyth.

"Get up here and enjoy this sunrise," Janet yelled down. "I won fair and square."

"Don't rub it in, Janet," Scott yelled back. He took a deep breath and rode up to the top of the hill.

Below was a long, twisting valley with a wooded bottom and slopes of tall grass and sage: the Rosebud. Pine and cedar grew in thick patches among sandstone rocks and on red hills that the sun had turned crimson. The morning was clear, and the land seemed to stretch on forever.

"It's beautiful," said Janet. "Just beautiful."

"Who do you suppose that is?" Scott asked, pointing far out to a group of riders. "They must have come from the Little Wolf country."

Janet looked for a while then turned back to the valley below. "It's hard to say. With the roundups starting, it could be just about anybody."

Scott continued to watch them, little specks in the distance that weaved in a column from a high hill out of sight in the far reaches of timber. He shook his head.

"It's still a little early for roundup."

Janet turned her horse and started down the hill. "Let's go. Pa's no doubt waiting breakfast." She laughed again and turned back to Scott. "Want to race to see who does the dishes?"

"Forget it!"

It took the morning to reach the C Bar S. Scott had taken his time, thinking more of the fun Janet was probably having in town than the work ahead of him. It couldn't really be considered work, leading two mares, each a month along with foal, in a slow march down Rosebud Creek. The C Bar S had been good to them since they had first arrived, helping with roundup and the dreary line camp work through the winter months. Now the C Bar S was giving them these two older mares with foal in trade for Scott chopping firewood at two of their line camps. It was a more than fair trade. An outfit couldn't get by in this country without plenty of good horses.

Scott was happy that things were working out. They had been in southeastern Montana Territory for nearly two years, and their Circle 6 Cattle Company had grown faster than they had expected, though then they had had nothing more than a place to build a cabin and five hundred head of longhorns. Scott and Janet's pa just had them and a handful of hired cowboys who came at roundup time each spring. Their ma lay buried beneath the plains of Kansas, killed by the coughs, they said. Scott figured it was heartbreak from when his little sister, Lisa, drowned in the creek. None of them would really get over it, but their ma had felt it was her fault until the day she died.

A year passed, and all Kansas could bring was sad memories. Scott remembered how glad he had been the day his pa told him they were going north into the cattle country, to leave the plow behind and try something other folks were getting rich at. Scott kept thinking of what his pa was always saying about this being a new start and a new life. But somehow the past kept haunting them. The year Lisa had drowned, she had been given a two-year-old colt for Christmas. Their ma's last words had been for Janet to take care of that horse. Now the horse meant more to her than anything else in the world. He had grown to a big palomino with the dark gold of fall grass in the morning, and his mane was as white as the clouds in the sky. Janet had trained him to do anything she wanted, and now she was spending more time than ever with the horse. Maybe things would have been better if their ma were still alive, but Janet and her pa were having trouble getting along. They were too much alike.

Scott wasn't past hope for the future. Things would get better. This was cow country, the best you could find. Things would be good for them here. Just a couple of more years to build up the herd, and things would be real good.

When Scott rode into the C Bar S headquarters, he counted nearly twenty cowhands around the corrals, nearly the entire C Bar S roundup crew. Scott knew they weren't waiting for him.

"Where's your sister?" one of them yelled with disgust in his voice. "I thought Janet was supposed to pick up the mares."

"I raced her to see who got to go to town and who had to come up here," Scott answered. "I lost."

The cowboy looked at Scott a second and then said, "Shit." He jumped off the corral. The other hands followed close behind him to their horses, all grumbling to themselves, and were soon gone in a cloud of dust. Scott knew they would also be on their way to town. Roundup would begin in just a few days, and this would be their last chance for a good time. It amused Scott, for he knew they would have been gone a long time before this had they known Janet wasn't coming to the C Bar S to pick up the mares.

One of the C Bar S hands had stayed behind to help Scott with the mares. He tilted his hat and introduced himself as Gene Huntley. His smile creased a tanned face with piercing blue eyes set off by a heavy crop of dark hair.

"Everybody gets to go to town but you and me." He laughed. "This outfit just put me on to break horses, and there's a lot of them in that corral."

Huntley had been at the C Bar S less than a week, he told Scott. He seemed the typical hand who drifted in for the work each summer and then drifted out again in the fall. He was as independent as all the rest but had an easygoing manner that Scott liked; he seemed friendlier than most. Gene already seemed to know a lot about Scott and his family. That was easy to understand, for Janet was talked about in all the cow camps in the valley. In a country where women of any sort were scarce, she was a true novelty. And Scott himself was made to feel special when Gene told him that, twelve-years-old or not, it took a man to work cattle in this country.

"You should have seen how everybody got cleaned up for your sister this morning." Gene laughed. "Then you ruin everybody's day."

"I think it's funny," Scott replied. "They all hang around here to see Janet, and she don't even show up." He laughed. "Now I feel better about that race I lost."

Gene took a rope and stood near Scott, forming a noose. "I've heard a lot about both your sister and that horse of hers," he said. "Sounds like she's beaten everybody in the country."

"If I hear any more about that horse, I think I'll get sick."

Gene chuckled. "Let's get your mares."

Scott watched Gene carefully sort one of the mares from the other horses in the corral and swing his noose. He saw a flock of waxwings fly close overhead toward a grove of pines not far to the west. They started to land but broke up in midflight and veered off in all directions before regrouping to land in another stand farther down the hill. Scott continued to watch the hill.

"Leave them out on grass all summer and don't work them," Scott heard Gene saying. "Come about Christmastime, you'll have two fine colts."

Still watching the hill, Scott saw the waxwings break from the trees and fly over the corrals, scolding in a chorus of high, buzzlike calls.

Gene then led the mare to where Scott sat on the corrals. "What's the matter, Scott?"

"Look at that." Scott was pointing to a group of riders coming down from the pines to the west on a dead run.

Gene climbed the corrals beside Scott. "Now, who the hell are they?" He jumped to the ground, pulling Scott with him. "Head for the barn. They've got rifles!"

Scott and Gene dove inside just as a bullet splintered the wood of the door. Through a crack in the log wall, Scott watched them open the corral gates and herd all the horses out.

"Horse thieves!" Gene hissed. "Goddamnit!"

"Let's get them two inside," one of the riders yelled. He jumped from his horse and came toward the barn on a run.

Scott saw an older man with a patchy gray beard wave his gun at the man and yell, "Forget it! We ain't got the time!"

But the other man wasn't listening. He jumped through the doorway of the barn, his eyes wild and his head moving in jerky motions to try to find Scott and Gene.

"Don't move," Gene whispered calmly to Scott. "Hunch down here and don't move."

Scott crouched deeper into the shadows along the log wall and then slid in under a feed trough. Gene carefully inched his way from behind the trough away from Scott. From the corrals came the sounds of voices and of a hundred hooves pounding the ground outside the barn walls. Scott's heart was in his mouth; his hands clutched the edge of the wood trough until a numbness crept into his fingers. Then there were footsteps nearby and the roar of a Colt, once and then two and three times. There was the thunk of bullets into wood and then Gene scrambling. He heard a throaty laugh, and the footsteps came closer. The man was running. Scott sat frozen, unable to move. Above him was the horse thief, his eyes wide with surprise at seeing Scott.

Scott's nerves exploded, and he sprang from beneath the trough, yelling at the top of his lungs. He pushed out with all his might, sending the thief backward into the barn wall. Then came the blast from a Colt somewhere close behind him, and the thief's eyes widened. Two more shots, and the thief was yelling hoarsely and shooting into the ground.

"Scott, get down!" Gene was yelling as he emptied his Colt into the outlaw's body.

Scott stood paralyzed, watching the man twist and turn on the barn floor. He was only moaning now, and soon he lay still while the dust was a heavy haze in the sunlight that poured through the open door.

"God," said Scott, and sank to his knees.

Gene pushed him back under the feed trough. "Stay there," he ordered.

Scott heard him reload the Colt and step noisily to the door of the barn. Outside, there was silence. Gene stood at the door for what seemed to Scott an eternity. Then he made his way to a window and looked out in all directions. A slight wind had come up, and it was whistling through the cracks in the logs, swirling the heavy dust that still clogged the air inside. Finally, Gene motioned for him to follow.

Scott made his way around the body and followed Gene out the door. The wind was still coming in gusts, and far to the east was a cloud of dust that no doubt had been made by horses. Gene put his pistol back into its holster and kicked his boot through the dust with a loud curse. Scott watched him walk to the corrals and climb up, taking a seat. He put his head in his hands and gazed out across the empty space where the horses had gone. Barely twenty minutes before, the C Bar S had been a beehive of activity. There had been men and horses busily getting ready for roundup. Now the only sound was the creak of an empty corral gate swinging in the wind.

Chapter 2

Gene tied the dead man's horse—the only one left on the place—to a corral pole and went back inside the barn. Scott watched him drag the body out, leaving behind a large red blotch that had soaked into the dirt and loose hay of the floor. Scott choked and turned for a breath of fresh air.

"Not a pretty sight," Gene said to Scott. "Let's go sit down. There's nothing we can do now until the rest of the hands get back here. I'll lay odds they don't get far down the valley before they run into more trouble like this."

Scott sat in a daze. Everything seemed strange and unreal. He had already given some thought to what Gene had just said. What if these or other thieves had raided their own ranch? It brought a bad feeling to the pit of his stomach.

"I expect you're worried about your sister and your pa," said Gene. "Can't say as I blame you."

"Not so much Janet," Scott said. "She's in town. Besides, she can take care of herself. It's Pa. He's up in years, and if there was any bad trouble, he'd be in on the fight tooth and nail. I just don't know what to think. Maybe they didn't hit our place."

9

"The odds are they did, Scott. Just looking at the dust in the air, I'd say they hit everything this side of the reservation."

Scott shuddered. "Do you think they tried to kill everybody, like they did us?"

"Not likely. They wouldn't have time to do much more than steal the horses and get away fast. They wouldn't risk men in shootouts. The one who chased us into the barn was a fool."

"What if there was one like that when they hit our place?" Scott asked.

Gene shook his head. "I don't know, Scott."

Scott and Gene looked to the north, where another cloud of dust had built up and was approaching fast. Soon a large group of riders came into view. These, Scott knew, were the C Bar S hands, and it looked like they had men from the neighboring spreads with them. Gene had been right; the entire lower Rosebud valley had been hit.

Scott and Gene stood up as they dismounted. "Todd looks hopping mad," said Gene.

Todd was the cowhand who had said "Shit!" on seeing Scott instead of Janet earlier in the day. It was he who led the hands over to where they formed a semicircle around Scott and Gene.

"They wipe us out entirely?" he asked Gene.

Gene nodded. "About a half hour ago."

Todd cursed and slapped his gloves against his chaps. "We rode as hard as we could. Guess we didn't ride hard enough."

Scott looked among the group and recognized hands from all up and down the Rosebud and some from farther west. There was a large number of Sugar Bowl and 70L cowhands, with a few from the SH and FUF spreads. As Scott and Gene found out, the thieves had missed the FUF, one of the biggest horse ranches in the country, and the FUF was willing to supply horses until the other outfits got their own back.

"I see you got one of them," Todd said to Gene as he looked over to the corrals. "Are you ready to join us and get the rest of them?"

Gene shook his head. "That's not a good idea, Todd."

"What do you mean it's not a good idea? We can't stand to lose horses like this, any of us."

There was a loud sound of agreement from the other hands, and when they had settled down, Gene said, "That's not the kind of thing that will get our horses back. Men like that are used to people riding out after them half-cocked and hot under the collar. That way they can lead you into some hellhole and blast you all to bits. Besides, there's roundup work to do."

"Roundup work?" said Todd. "Without horses?"

"The FUF just offered horses," Gene reminded him. "Use them for roundup and let the law handle the thieves."

"The law?" Todd said. "What law? It'll be six months before we see a badge from any direction. We've got to handle this now!"

Again there was a roar of agreement. But Gene was still shaking his head.

"You boys just don't understand," he said. "There are a lot of things that can happen when a mob goes wild that most likely shouldn't."

Todd squinted. "What are you driving at?"

"The wrong men get hanged for one. You can bet on it. Somebody might be pushing his own stock somewhere and just happen to have a few along without his brand on them. A bunch of men show up looking for stolen horses, and things get twisted up to the point where an innocent man dies. You want that hanging over your heads?''

There was a short silence, and then Todd said, ''How do you know so much about it, Huntley?''

''Just take my word for it. Let someone who is cut out for it do that work. You stick to punchin' cows.''

''Maybe he's right,'' one of the other hands put in. ''Maybe we are better off to wait. I heard of someone who might do the job for us. I heard the White Bandit was in the country.''

There was silence. Scott saw the hands look to each other with wide eyes. Gene himself showed an expression of mild surprise.

''They say he was over Great Falls way not long ago,'' the hand went on, ''and that he was headed north for the Missouri badlands to chase thieves up there. When he hears about this, he'll be down and there'll be dead thieves scattered all the way from here to the Dakotas.''

''The White Bandit,'' said Todd. ''Is he the one the law is chasin'?''

''That's him.''

''Hell, he's more outlaw than them damn thieves!''

''Maybe, but he's a good regulator. The ranchers pay him, and he gets rid of thieves, no questions asked.''

''Nobody even knows for sure who he is,'' Todd went on. ''He's like a ghost. Maybe he don't even exist.''

The hand quickly said, ''Oh, he exists, all right. He's for damn sure real.''

Scott looked to Gene and saw that he was staring out over the valley.

''Huntley,'' Todd said, ''you heard anything about him?''

"Just the same stories you have," Gene answered. "I say we leave the manhunt business to somebody like him."

Todd and the other hands murmured among themselves. Gene motioned Todd over to the dead man's horse. "I'll take Scott back down to his place on that horse," he said. "It would be best if you and the rest of the boys took up the FUF offer to borrow horses. At least until after roundup."

Todd looked to the other hands. "Maybe we'd best head into town like we planned and get our supplies." He turned back to Gene. "You haven't got any horses to break now, Huntley."

"I'll find plenty to do," Gene told him. "Maybe I'll meet you boys later."

When they had left, Scott followed Gene over to the horse and watched him climb on. A feeling of dread at what he might find at home came over him, mixed with hope that things might turn out all right.

"When do you think he'll come, Gene?" Scott asked. "The one they call the White Bandit."

Gene held his hand down and pulled Scott up behind him on the horse, answering slowly and in an easy manner. "You never know about men like that, Scott. They come and they go. He may show up; he may not."

"But he always comes at times like this. Isn't that what they say about him?"

"Stories are a dime a dozen, Scott. Good or bad, don't always put your faith in them."

The sun was just above the horizon, giving off a soft light that soaked into the red rock on the hills and set them off from the green of the pines and the spring grass. Scott would have called it a pretty sight any other time. But now, as he and Gene rode slowly down the hill toward the ranch yard, all he could see was three horses in a corral that had held thirty that morning and a man standing in the doorway of their cabin, holding a rifle.

Gene pulled the horse to a stop and yelled, "We're not thieves. I've brought Scott back."

The man lowered the rifle and waved them in. He was a short, heavily built man with a graying beard, and Scott noticed a stethoscope around his neck.

"Can't be too careful," he said.

The inside of the cabin smelled of medicine, and Scott stood unable to speak when he saw his pa lying on his bunk under a pile of blankets, deep in a drugged sleep.

"I just finished working on him," the doctor told Scott. He held up a large sliver of bone in a pair of tweezers. "He was hit in the leg with a slug from a Sharps buffalo rifle. He's a strong one or he wouldn't be alive now."

Scott finally managed to speak. "He won't die now, will he?"

"Not if he stays quiet," the doctor answered. "He'll be off that leg a long time, but he'll live. His femur was shattered, and it will shorten his leg some, so he'll have to get used to things being different for him. Just keep him quiet."

Scott knelt down beside his pa, and tears welled in his eyes. He bit his lip hard and took a deep breath.

Gene moved next to him and put a hand on his shoulder. "It's been a rough day," he told Scott. "You're doin' pretty good."

Scott cleared his throat and turned to the doctor. "What about my sister? Have you heard anything about Janet?"

The doctor nodded. "One of your hands told me she

had gone off after a horse the thieves had stolen or something of the kind. I can't imagine that. But then, I don't know your sister.''

"That sounds like her," said Scott. He shook his head. "What else can happen?"

"Your hands are out looking for horses that may have gotten loose from the thieves," the doctor went on. "They found those three in the corral down near the creek. They figured maybe others got loose somewhere else along the line." He picked up his black bag. "I've got to go. There are people shot up all over this country." He turned when he reached the door. "Give him the medicine I left every four hours. It'll keep him still."

Scott and Gene went to the door and watched the doctor leave. The sun had fallen behind the horizon, and the sky was a deep crimson. The blazing sunset seemed to run the entire length of the western sky, and the tops of the pines looked jagged and black along the hilltops.

"Look at that sky," said Gene. "I'd lay odds we get a change in weather. Cold. Maybe even snow."

Already a cool breeze had come in from the west, just a whisper. But far out, moving into the sunset, was a line of dark clouds.

"I think I'll take a quick look around the corrals before it gets dark," Gene said. "Maybe we can get an idea who these thieves are."

Scott went back inside and struck light to a lantern. He looked over to the bunk where his pa lay, and his mind turned over what he should do. Janet had gone off after her horse, and it was anybody's guess where she would end up. Although there were no horses left for roundup, it was possible the hands could borrow from the FUF, as the other outfits in the country were doing. He went to the door and looked to where Gene was studying tracks in the dust near the barn. The three horses the hands had found were milling and snorting in the corral, still unsettled from the raid earlier in the day. Scott shook his head and turned back inside the cabin.

When Gene came back from the corrals, Scott was filling a saddlebag with food. The sun was gone, and the light from the lantern cast dancing shadows on the wall.

"Looks like you plan on a trip someplace," Gene said.

"I don't have a choice," Scott replied. "Janet's run off, Pa can't even move, and we've got three horses to our name."

"What about your pa?"

"I left a note for the hands. They can take care of him as well as or better than me."

Gene shuffled his feet. "Can you do much alone?"

"I've got to go," Scott insisted. "It's not so much the horses. I've got to find Janet before she does something crazy. I just hope I can find her. This is a powerful big country to have to find somebody in."

"You got any idea where she's headed?"

"Not really. I doubt if she does, either."

After a moment Gene asked, "You mind if I tag along?"

Scott blinked with surprise.

"I sort of feel responsible for those horses we lost and those two mares we promised you."

"None of what happened today was your fault, Gene. The C Bar S won't hold you to blame."

"I know," said Gene. "Still, I can't just ride away from all this. Without horses to break, I'm out of a job. I planned to set out after those horses. I just figured the two of us together would make more sense than each alone—that is, if you're agreeable."

Scott finished filling his saddlebag and tied down the flap. "What if Janet won't turn back? What if she wants to chase the horse thieves?"

"We'll worry about that when the time comes," Gene told him. "The best thing we can do now is get some sleep. We've got a long trip ahead of us."

While Gene brought his bedroll in and laid it out on the floor, Scott gave his pa more medicine and got his own bunk arranged. He blew out the lantern and lay back, looking up into the darkness and wondering whether all this was real. Then Gene's voice broke the stillness.

"Can you shoot a pistol, Scott?"

"I've mostly shot rifles," he answered. "Pa don't like me fooling around with handguns. But I reckon I could shoot one good enough."

"I don't intend to get you into a shootout if I can help it," Gene said. "But that's a chance you'd take ridin' with me or alone. I just figure it pays to be ready."

"I've never shot at a man before," Scott said with a hint of anger in his voice. "But after today, I think I could get used to it mighty easy."

Chapter 3

Janet was something to look at. Like Gene's blue eyes and dark hair, her brown eyes brought out the red in her sandy features. She was a full ten years older than Scott, but the two were as close as brother and sister could be.

Since coming up to Montana Territory, the Nolans had met nearly every cowhand on the northern plains. All looking for work, they said, but all looking hard at Janet while they talked. She gave none of them anything to come back for except maybe a Saturday night dance. She never saw a one that interested her in the least—that is until Scott and Gene crossed the Tongue River and found her boiling coffee at a JO Ranch line cabin.

It was a surprise to find her there in the middle of all that country. It was also a case of blind luck. Scott had suggested warming up, for the wind was raw, and the JO line cabin had only been a few miles out of their way.

"I'm not going back without Clipper, Scott. And that's final."

Scott got down from his horse. "Who said anything about going back?"

"Pa sent you, didn't he?"

"No."

"He thought you could talk me into going back."

"No, I came by myself. Pa would like as not skin me alive if he had hold of me now. But you should know, he got himself shot up."

"What?"

"He's lucky he didn't lose his right leg. A doctor down from Miles City worked on him most of the morning. He said Pa will be laid up for a long spell but that he'll pull through."

Janet was relieved. She filled tin cups with coffee and offered one to both Scott and Gene. She took a quick sip of coffee and straightened the leg on her riding dress.

"You must be a new hand with one of the neighbors," she said to Gene.

"I took a job breaking horses for the C Bar S."

"You lose horses?"

"We lost them all."

"How did you hear about the raid, Janet?" Scott asked.

"Some M Diamond cowhands told us on the road," she answered. "They said all of Rosebud Creek got hit hard and that we got cleaned out. I borrowed a horse from them and started out. I guess I don't know the country too well."

"Why didn't you come back up to the ranch?" Scott asked. "How did you expect to get Clipper back by yourself?"

"Don't preach to me, Scott," Janet said, flashing her eyes. "You're not old enough to even be out here."

"At least I know the country," Scott said.

"He must be some horse," Gene said to Janet.

"He is."

"Is he worth getting killed over?"

"Mr. Huntley, Clipper and I have been through a lot together. I don't intend to lose him now." She moved off by herself.

"Maybe we should go on by ourselves," Scott suggested. "She's pretty upset."

Gene sipped his coffee. "Let's wait. She wouldn't do anything crazy, though, would she?"

"No. Sometimes she acts like an old-lady badger, but she won't get crazy."

They got ready to leave, and Janet mounted her borrowed mare. She gave the horse a gentle pat, but it was easy to tell that she wished she still had Clipper.

Scott led them up and out of the cottonwoods along the river and into pine-covered ridges and grassy parklands. It would be slow going until they broke into the rolling sage hills of the Powder River country. There was a good trail, and it looked like the thieves were headed for the badlands along the lower Yellowstone, heading into that country the back way to avoid unnecessary trouble. It fit. The country due south of them was full of troopers and settlers, and Canada was at least a hard week's ride to the north across two major rivers that were sure to be swollen with the spring runoff. The country they were in now was the safest place to travel for nearly a hundred miles both ways if you didn't want to run into a lot of people with the authority to ask questions.

They pushed hard and stopped only to water the horses. If they wanted their horses back, they had to catch them in the open Powder River country before they reached the badlands; there was no other way to look at it. Once they got into the badlands, the going would be three times as tough. Following a trail would be even worse. A place like that is full of little canyons and holes that can hold a hundred head of horses without anyone ever knowing. One storm could wipe out any trail that had been made. After that a man could spend weeks just going in circles.

Night came in, and though the moon was big and bright, it wasn't much help in lighting the trail through the timber. If they pushed on, they would stand a good chance of losing the trail completely. And there was the worry of losing time. But it was certain the thieves would have to stop and graze the horses sooner or later. Since they were this far out into the hills, the chances were better than even that they would choose this night.

Scott finished his meal and settled in under a wool blanket. The light the moon had made was beginning to fade, and a dark curtain of clouds was filling the sky. While Scott watched as the stars became lost in the black, Gene and Janet sat near the fire, sharing a can of beans. When they had finished, Gene sat down with his pistol and began to clean it.

"How did you happen to join up with Scott in this?" Janet asked.

Gene pulled a spare pistol out of his saddlebag and got set to clean it. "Scott and I were alone at the C Bar S when the thieves hit. I killed one of them when he chased us into the barn. I took Scott home, and we decided to ride together."

"I see," said Janet. "Wasn't there anybody else from the C Bar S willing to ride with you?"

Gene worked at his gun. "I talked them out of it. I was responsible for the horses; it should be me who gets them back. Aren't you wasting good sleep time?"

Janet left it at that and went over to where the wood

was piled. "I think I'll build the fire up a little. I'm not that tired."

"Just don't use it all so we waste time chopping more for breakfast," Gene said.

"I'll get my own," she said curtly. She grabbed Gene's hatchet and tromped into the woods.

In a minute she was in the darkness outside of camp, snapping branches and chopping fallen logs. She came back with enough wood for two days and dropped it all in a heap near the fire. The flames licked up over the abundance of new fuel and changed from yellow to red as they worked to fill the space between logs. The wind came up and helped, turning the bottom coals a deep glowing red and making the whole works pop and shoot sparks.

Content with her work, Janet got up and found a tree to lean against. There was silence as the fire played merrily in its little spot on the ground, dancing up and down and around as gusts of wind seeped through the timber into camp.

Gene's gun clicked as he worked with it. "Acts like a storm is moving in," he said, breaking the silence.

Janet was looking into the fire, pretending she hadn't heard him.

"I guess I should apologize," Gene said. "There was no call for me to be unneighborly."

"We're all pretty edgy," she said. "Scott's the only smart one here. We're both sitting up fighting each other like a couple of fools when we should be resting up for the real enemy."

"There's no doubt about that," Gene replied. "Just so I don't have any more enemies than the ones we're after."

Janet turned to him and met his grin. "I promise you're not an enemy. How about me?"

"Anybody that can chop wood like you can is definitely on my side."

Janet laughed. "I'm not always that efficient."

"I don't know," said Gene, putting the Colt back into his saddlebag and pulling out a box of cartridges. "But I would say if you get as riled at those thieves as you did here, they won't stand a chance."

Janet turned serious again. "We've got to find them. We've just got to look and look until we find them."

Gene pushed .44 cartridges into the loops in his gun belt. "There's always other horses. You only got one life."

She got up and moved over to the fire. "One life," she said, huddling down near the flames. "One life of what? Being alone, playing games with people, watching everyone step on each other to get rich. Watching the good, honest people in this world lose out—and nobody caring. That tops it all; nobody cares. No, I don't think life is worth more to me than Clipper."

"Maybe you need a change. Have you ever thought of moving back east? Or maybe south? Could be this country life is tying you down."

Janet shook her head. "Believe me, Mr. Huntley, that's not it. I just want my horse back." She got up and began to move her bedroll close to the fire.

Gene watched her a moment and said, "I hope you don't plan to bed down there."

"Why not?"

"If you think you'll get cold, I've got an extra blanket. You may as well use it." He got up and went over to his own bedroll.

"I'll be just fine here, thank you," Janet said.

"Take the blanket and move back where you were," Gene insisted. "The sparks are flyin' thick in this wind. There's one fire in camp already. We don't need you for a second.'' He tossed the blanket down away from the fire and went back to work on his Winchester.

Janet moved her bedroll back from the fire and hesitated beside the blanket. ''Won't you need it?'' she asked.

''No. One's about all I ever use.''

Janet studied Gene a moment and then settled into her bedroll and wrapped herself tightly in the blankets. She lay staring up at the sky for a short time and then took a deep breath and rolled over on her side. In a moment she was asleep.

Gene finished cleaning the Winchester and put it back in its scabbard near his bedroll. He found a bottle of whiskey and went back over to the fire. After a swallow from the bottle, he reached into a pocket and pulled out an empty shell casing. He took another drink from the bottle and studied the shell closely, his face deepening into a dark frown.

Scott crawled out of his bedroll and came over, seating himself next to Gene by the fire.

Gene looked up in surprise. ''I thought you were asleep.''

Scott shrugged and warmed his hands over the fire. ''I'm not really tired.''

''You'd better sleep while you can,'' Gene advised him. ''We may not get a chance like this again.''

''I guess I'm too wound up about all this. I just can't relax.''

Gene nodded. ''A lot has happened to you in a short time. Things will work out, though.''

''I sure hope so. We need those horses back bad. We can't run our spread without them. And it would be a shame to lose Clipper. He's the best horse in the world, even if he is Janet's.''

''Sounds like you wish he was yours.''

"Janet promised me the first colt out of him, that is, if we ever get him back." Scott shuffled a bit. "Janet really loves that horse."

Gene tipped the bottle again and said, "You've got more on your mind than Janet's horse, I'd say."

Scott nodded and looked into the fire, biting his lip and twisting his hands in front of him.

"Worried about your pa?"

"Some. I keep thinking about him, lyin' still on that bunk and all full of medicine."

"A hard thing to push out of your mind." Gene held the bottle out to Scott. "Try this. It'll settle you down."

"Maybe I'll have just a little. Just so Pa doesn't find out."

Gene smiled. "I won't tell."

Scott took a gulp from the bottle. The whiskey stung on the way down, and Scott turned his head so that Gene wouldn't see the water in his eyes. He muffled a cough and handed the bottle back.

Gene reached into his saddlebag and pulled out a single-action Colt .44, which he handed to Scott. "Keep this in your belt, just in case. The hammer is on an empty chamber." He also gave Scott a handful of cartridges. "Don't lose these. And remember, you only have five shots."

Scott felt the cold steel in his hands. It gleamed in the light of the fire. He had often used a pistol to pot prairie dogs with the hands from the ranch. He had gotten pretty good and could keep a steady aim. Now he trembled at the thought of turning it on a man.

"I'll use it if I have to," he told Gene firmly.

Scott took another drink from the bottle, a smaller one that rolled down his throat and sent a warmness creeping over him. He noticed Gene looking at the rifle casing again with that same frown on his face.

"What have you got there?" he asked Gene.

"It's a shell from a .50-caliber Sharps, Scott." Gene pointed to a small speck of red paint on the side of the casing. "This belongs to a man named Taggert. Old Man Taggert, they call him. The red paint on the casing is his trademark. I found this in the dirt near your corrals last night."

Scott took another swallow from the bottle. He stared at the casing. "Is he the one who shot Pa?"

Gene nodded. "He's the head of a big family of cutthroats. They were hide hunters until the buffalo ran out a few years back. Now they peddle rotgut whiskey to the Indians and steal other people's horses."

"You know him personal or something?" Scott asked.

Gene's eyes were directed to the fire, and they were dark and hard. "They killed two of my brothers a year and a half ago just for a load of lousy buffalo hides."

"You've got more at stake in this than just getting C Bar S horses back."

Gene rolled the empty casing between his thumb and forefinger. "I reckon I do for a fact."

Suddenly the wind came up strong and whipped the fire into a crazy dance. Raindrops cold as ice began falling in Scott's face.

"Let's get some sleep," Gene said. "We're headed for a hard time from here on out."

Scott crawled back into his bedroll. The feeling that things were unreal came on stronger than ever, and he swallowed hard at the dryness that had touched the back of his throat. The wind had come in stronger, and the raindrops stung like tiny nails. The trees rustled in their tops, and here and there one would moan and creak as it swayed.

As suddenly as it had come up, the wind died out altogether. The air filled with giant snowflakes that floated against the skin and made a cool wetness. A calm settled in the camp, and the night turned quiet. Tomorrow the hills would have a blanket of snow. It would be a pretty sight to see in the early light, but it would hide the trail the thieves had made. Without a trail to follow, the odds of getting the horses back were stacked against them. Somehow that didn't seem to matter. With Janet looking for her horse and Gene looking for his brothers' killers, Scott knew he was riding with two people who would never give up.

Chapter 4

Gene woke Scott and Janet before daylight. It had snowed three to four inches, and the ground was wet and heavy. The air was still cold and damp from the storm, and it was hard to get rid of the shivers even after a bellyfull of hot coffee.

They broke camp after the coffee and more warmed-up beans. It wasn't much more than something to pep them up and get them going. There would probably be no more stopping for the rest of their journey, and the food would be cold from now on. The eastern sky was graying fast, and the tree-lined ridges had taken on the look of a vast, black ocean with crooked, sharp-tipped waves. The snow clung to the ground like a thick, wet blanket, and the still air was broken only by the plod of horses' hooves and the squeak of wet leather.

They hit the slopes above Pumpkin Creek just as the sun topped into full view. The light picked out the gurgling water and set off the ups and downs in the current. The willows and brush along the banks stood white-humped as they followed the curves and twists of the creek bed. A lone coyote trotted along a trail through the sagebrush, keeping to the edge of the

28

shadows and stopping now and again to test the air with his nose.

The timber was getting more patchy, and the hills broke out rounder and with more meadow between them. The snow had done a good job of covering the trail of the thieves and stolen horses, but there wasn't time to fret over it. It was certain now that the thieves were headed for the badlands, and the only thing to do was to try to catch up with them somehow.

Overhead the sky was deep blue, but there was a gray haze forming in the west, the kind that usually means rain later in the day. The air was getting a nice, warm feel to it, and on the slopes where the sun hit directly, little patches of bare ground were starting to show.

Pumpkin Creek was gurgling and murky, as was to be expected that time of year. But it carried a lot more dirt than normal, which meant there was a pretty good amount of runoff water from the snow. It pointed out a major concern for them. There was still a lot of country to cover before they hit the Powder River, one of the major tributaries of the Yellowstone. No doubt the snow was a lot heavier farther south in the Big Horn Mountains, where the headwaters formed. It could mean a lot of problems getting across, or it could mean not getting across at all.

They let the horses ease into a gentle lope east of Pumpkin Creek, slowing them every two miles or so. They had to make fast time, yet the last thing they wanted was to play the horses out and end up walking. They had to do it right and hope they could cross the Powder River; otherwise, they had all just gone on a hard ride in the snow for nothing.

They had been riding for nearly six hours when they came upon a lone set of tracks. It was getting near midday, and the sun was settling the snow in a hurry. They knew that the tracks were fresh because they hadn't settled.

Gene frowned. "Can't figure any cowhands traveling alone way out here off the beaten track." He checked both his Colt and his saddle gun.

Scott checked the pistol Gene had given him. The steel was still cold, and the cold crept through him to the bone. They got off their horses to stretch and study the tracks. At first they thought one of the thieves had doubled back and was on his way to tell the rest that they were being followed. But the horse was traveling at a steady lope, not the dead run of someone in a hurry. Maybe he was being crafty. In any case, there wasn't any doubt the rider was out there for the same reason they were. It just remained to be seen which side of the cause he was on.

They mounted and moved on. Once again, big patches of timber started cropping up on the ridges. The tension within was building steadily now that they knew the thieves couldn't be that far ahead; knowing that someone was up ahead and could easily be waiting to train a rifle on them made it that much worse.

Gene used every trick he knew to stay on the trail yet avoid being set up for an ambush. Going through little gullies and around ridges surrounded by pines kept their eyes wide open and their blood running fast. But Gene had the right idea. It was better to find out as soon as possible who it was and where he stood rather than forgetting about it and maybe dying as a result. Besides, the tracks were headed the same direction they wanted to go, and whoever was making them couldn't have picked his trails and creek crossings any better.

It was midafternoon when they hit the Mizpah. They crossed it fairly easily, since it wasn't that long compared with most of the major streams in the country. Even so, the water was a darker shade than Pumpkin Creek had been, which meant there wasn't a lot of time before the Powder River would be too high to cross.

Late day brought a change in the air. Whispers of wind breathed cool against their faces. Soon a gray haze crept in from the west and settled into thick clouds that were dark on the bottom. A storm now would do them no good; it would only make the going rougher.

Their minds were set on making time. They had crossed the Mizpah, and the Powder River was not far off. They were easing their horses down a small, timbered draw when someone spoke from the hillside above them.

"A good afternoon to you."

They looked up into the bore of a Spencer .52 repeater. A crop of silver-tinged hair and a grizzled beard stuck out from under a trail-worn derby.

"Is it Taggert?" Scott asked Gene.

Gene shook his head no. "I don't know who it is."

The rider leaned the Spencer over the saddle in front of him. His words had an edge.

"Any reason you three should be travelin' this country?"

"Trailin' horse thieves," Gene answered. "Guess we found one."

The rider grunted. "You should be careful about name-callin' in this country."

"You haven't said anything that would change my mind," Gene answered.

"I figure to be the one askin' the questions," the stranger said. "Now, why would just three of you be way out here after a whole bunch of horse thieves?"

"There could be more than just three of us," Gene answered.

The rider shook his head. "No. There's just you three." He leaned back in his saddle and arched the Spencer back over his shoulder to point. "A man can see a long ways from this high hill behind me. I've had my eye on you for close to an hour now."

"We were in a hurry," said Gene. "I should have known about that hill."

The rider nodded with a little grin on his face. "I've got to hand it to you, though. You skirted those draws and timber stands like an Indian scout. It appears you've done some trackin' in your time."

"Maybe a little."

"A lot," the rider said, correcting him. "You've done a lot of trackin' in your time. And you learned it pretty good. But I've got the drop on you, and I need some answers to some questions."

Janet spoke up. "Maybe you haven't got as much of a drop on us as you think you have." She turned her horse and started up the hill toward him.

"What's on your mind, little lady?" he asked, lifting the Spencer off the saddle.

Janet pulled up next to him and said, "I can't decide if you're a thief or if you fit in with us, but I intend to find out right now." She pulled the glove off her shooting hand and grabbed her Winchester.

"Hold on," said the rider.

Janet had the Winchester out and was levering a round into the barrel. "You've been doing a lot of talking. Now it's time to see if you can back it up."

"Ease up, I'm not a thief!" He held the barrel of the Spencer up in the air and put out his free hand to stop her.

Janet lowered her rifle. "I like to get to the point right away. Now I know whose side you're on."

"You could have got your fool head blowed off," said the rider in disgust.

"Or you," Janet came back. "I'm more than a little upset over losing a horse I think the world of. Can you understand that, Mr. whoever you are?"

"Starky. Just call me Starky."

"Well, Mr. Starky?"

"Just Starky. No Mr. to it. Nothing personal, ma'am. I just didn't know."

"That's Janet," Gene told Starky. "She's a gun-fighter."

Starky looked at Janet and chuckled. "I won't argue with that."

Janet put the Winchester back into its scabbard. "I have nothing against you, either, Mr. Starky. I just don't like horse thieves, that's all."

"I'm convinced," said Starky. "How many head did you lose?"

"Nearly thirty head," Janet answered. "And Gene's outfit lost over fifty."

"What's your stake in this?" Gene asked.

Starky pulled his coat back, exposing a star on his chest. "I don't like horse thieves either," he said. "But that's not the main reason I'm here. I've been after one particular thief for a long time. Maybe you've heard of him. He's called the White Bandit."

Scott's eyes got big, and he looked at Gene. "He's the one the C Bar S hands talked about."

Starky looked at Gene. "You know him?"

Gene adjusted his hat. "Everybody knows him, don't they?"

"What I mean is, I heard he was seen down in these parts."

"Well, we're after horse thieves," Janet said. "And the White Bandit doesn't steal horses."

"I know he's a folk hero in these parts," Starky said. "And maybe he does more good than harm. But he takes the law into his own hands, and that ain't justice the way it's written down in this country."

"Maybe justice isn't written right," Janet said.

"That don't matter. I've got a warrant. I'm obliged to serve it."

"You serve your warrant," Gene said. "We've got horse thieves to catch."

"Maybe you didn't get the picture," Starky said. "You folks aren't the law, either."

Janet fumed. "I thought I made it clear to you, Mr. Starky, that nothing is going to stand between me and getting my horse back. Maybe we should both take our rifles back out."

There was a heavy silence. Finally Gene said, "I would judge you've been a lawman long enough to know that a badge is as good or bad as the man that wears it. You'd be a liar if you told any one of us that you always did your job by the book."

"I reckon that's true," Starky said. "But I've always worked in the name of justice."

"That's no doubt true," said Gene. "But you've learned to make changes now and then to get the job done. Otherwise, you'd be wearin' that star out on your coat instead of under it."

"You've got a point," said Starky. "I reckon I can't stop you. But if you was to let me ride with you, maybe things would be easier for all of us. Another lawman might not see things as clear as I do."

"You could deputize us," Janet said. "That's written in the books, isn't it?"

Starky chuckled. "It's written in the books."

Scott looked up at the sky. Little drops of rain were starting to fall, and Scott knew that time was getting more critical by the moment. It didn't bother him as much as it might have, for as they all put their slickers on, he felt that their luck would be good. The addition of Starky to their group was like a breath of fresh air, and it seemed to have the same effect on Gene and Janet.

"We'd better get on to the Powder River," Gene said. "It's bound to be hard crossing it now, and with more bad weather we may stand a chance of not crossing at all."

It was an hour's ride, and the going was tough, as the ground was gumbo. The storm had settled in, and the rain was coming steadily. It wasn't a downpour, but it was fairly heavy, the type of storm that might let up at any time or that could last for days. There was no doubt it would cause the snow to melt rapidly and come pouring off the hillsides into the streams and rivers. The Powder River would be a raging hell.

Chapter 5

They made the Powder River with two hours of daylight left. The rain had lessened considerably, but the damage had already been done. The river was swollen and rising steadily.

Scott led them downriver to where he knew there was a good crossing. Then, as they neared a line of cottonwoods that marked the crossing, he held them up and pointed through the rain with wide eyes. Strung out among the trees just ahead was a good-sized bunch of horses with men on horseback trying to get them into the river.

"My God, it's them!" Janet blurted out the words.

Scott felt his stomach squeeze into a tight knot. The cold in the air was nothing compared to what he felt inside. The time had come. He could see the same feeling in Janet's eyes. She was strong, but this would take something special. Gene had determination in his eyes, and Starky's eyes held a question.

"We've got to be sure about this," said Starky. "I know what it looks like, but we've got to be sure."

"Have you got a spyglass?" Gene asked.

Starky took one from his saddlebag, and Gene studied the running, squealing herd and the men who were desperately trying to push them into the roaring river.

"They're no friends of ours," he told Starky. "I see a lot of horses with different brands on them, all from the Rosebud. And I don't know a one of those men pushing them. We know what we have to do."

"Maybe we should wait until it's dark and try to get the jump on them," Starky suggested. "I count eight to ten riders. I don't like the odds, even if we could all shoot with the best of them."

Gene pulled his saddle gun and leaned over it to keep the rain off. "What if they join up with another group on the other side? Maybe you think we should try our luck with two or three times that many."

Starky took a deep breath and turned to Janet. "You sounded real good back there before noon," he said. "Can you handle this?"

"I'll do whatever I have to," Janet answered. "I didn't come along to watch."

He turned to Scott, who had taken the Colt from his belt. "What about you?"

Scott gripped the pistol so tightly that his knuckles turned white. "Don't forget, they're my horses too."

"We've got surprise on our side," said Gene. "That counts for a lot."

Starky pulled his Spencer and reached for cartridges in his saddlebag. "Maybe you're right."

"Two of us can go up this brushy draw and circle around them," Gene suggested. "If we can get at them from two sides, we'll have a big advantage. They won't know who we are in this rain."

Scott went with Starky, while Janet followed Gene up the brushy draw. It would take some time for them to get around on the other side of the thieves, and Starky took the opportunity to bolster Scott's courage.

"Stay calm, that's the key," he said. "Don't lose your head no matter what you see or hear. A man who can't keep control can't aim. And that's the man who'll die."

Scott nodded. "I'll remember that."

"There's no need to get into this unless you absolutely have to. Just take a stand somewhere and stay put. If you stay put and don't move, you'll get along fine."

"What if one of them sees me?"

"Just find some good cover. They'll have to come to you, and you'll have the odds in your favor." He gave Scott's shoulder a firm squeeze. "You'll do just fine."

Scott nodded. "I'll remember that."

Starky levered a round into the barrel of his Spencer. "I'll go out a ways and give you the edge of the river. Good luck."

Starky moved off and left Scott alone. The rain and the river drove hard at his ears, and he squeezed tight on the butt of the Colt .45 under his slicker. It was just him now, and the sound of the snorting horses and shouting men told him the time had come when he would learn what it was like to kill or be killed. He would learn how men make their own laws in a land with no formal order—just the law of the gun.

Scott had gone a short distance when a small group of horses came crashing through the trees and brush. They snorted in surprise when they saw him and then bolted past on a dead run. They were scattered enough that Scott could read brands. He read two Sugar Bowl and three SH brands for sure, and there were others. There was no doubt these men were thieves.

Then someone was shouting to him from just off to his left: "Why in hell didn't you stop those horses?"

The thief rode up beside Scott, and his face went

blank with surprise. Scott's hand froze on his gun. The thief got off two quick shots that went wild as his horse went out of control. Scott heard one of the bullets go past his left ear. With a deep breath, Scott held his horse steady and leveled his .45 for a quick shot as the thief turned to leave. The blast took the man high on the left side just above the last rib.

The thief gasped heavily, and his eyes rolled wide as he flopped backward off his horse. He landed on his back as the horse bolted into the trees and brush. Scott turned from the sight and left while the thief made his last jerks of life in the mud.

Scott breathed heavy; it seemed to keep his mind clear and help fight off the shock. He was in the trees now, near the water's edge. There were horses everywhere in the river, struggling to cross the swift water. Two of the horses had men on them, holding on tightly while the muddy current tried to pull them from their saddles. Scott thought he heard gunfire somewhere close by. The rolling water was deafening, and Scott strained his ears to hear any more shots. They were just a faint popping, and it was impossible to see where they were coming from.

Scott got off his horse and moved into a heavy stand of brush along the bank. Somewhere just ahead, something was happening in the river. He couldn't see for the slight bend in the course of the water and the heavy stand of trees along the bank, but he could hear shouting intermixed with gunfire.

On the opposite shore, Scott could see a huge man yelling and waving his arms at the men in the river. He dwarfed his own horse as if it were a small burro. It looked like he was telling someone on Scott's side of the river to hurry across and forget the horses. A massive load of hair and beard stuck out from under

some sort of fur cap. Even though the rain was falling
heavily again, Scott could see that the giant man's hair
was a brilliant red.

Scott remembered what Starky had said about staying tight in the brush. He tied his horse to a small
cottonwood at the edge of his hiding place and settled
back to wait. In a moment, five more stolen horses
rushed past. Close behind was a rider who stopped
when he saw Scott's horse. With a puzzled look, he
peered into the brush where Scott was crouched.

Scott could feel his heart pounding as fast as the
river. Stay calm, he told himself over and over. Just
stay calm. He again took the big Colt from his
waistband and cocked the trigger.

Suddenly the thief realized that he was looking into
the brush at two eyes with a hat over them and into a
face he didn't recognize. As the thief went for his gun,
Scott took steady aim, parting the brush with the barrel
of the pistol. Blue smoke belched from the brush, and
the thief doubled over at the middle and slid from his
horse.

Scott stood up in his hiding place, ready to fire again
while the thief tried to get to his feet. When the thief
gained his knees, Scott fired. The bullet tore through
the man's collarbone and into his throat. Scott was glad
the river had drowned out his voice, for it looked like
he was screaming.

The thief slumped forward and jerked momentarily
before lying still. He had lost his hat, and his face was
all blood from choking. Scott gagged and sank to his
knees. He made his fumbling fingers reload the pistol
and put it back in his waistband; the hot barrel burned
the skin on his stomach. Then he untied his horse and
took one last look at the dead outlaw. Scott knew that
he couldn't be too many years older than himself.

Out away from the river, the whole area seemed

alive with gunfire. The sun had pushed farther down, and the light in the trees was beginning to get dim. The shadow length was growing longer all the time, and making out faces was going to be a problem. From the way things sounded, a person could get shot in the time it took to look twice.

Scott urged his horse ahead through the trees and undergrowth, holding his breath for someone to appear. He had kept his composure in good fashion after ten minutes of killing for the first time. The worst part of it was that he knew things weren't all said and done yet. The sound of men and horses bearing down on him from just ahead brought his thoughts back to reality.

Scott moved his buckskin into a nearby stand of wild plum and waited. Three riders went by him as fast as they could make their horses go through the brush. Aside from not wanting to do any more shooting, Scott knew that he would stand little chance against all three of them. He sat tight while they went by. They were about thirty feet past him when the one in the rear fell off his horse.

One of the others came back and jumped off his horse. "Casey's hurt bad," he yelled.

The other man turned in his saddle. "We ain't got time for him. Let's get the hell across the river."

The wounded man got up to his hands and knees and begged not to be left.

"Are you comin' with me?" yelled the one on the horse.

"Rico, he ain't dead yet," said the man on the ground. "He can cross the river behind me on my horse."

"He'll never make it across."

"I can't leave him; he's my brother," the man on the ground was shouting, lifting his fallen brother by the armpits. "We've got to try!"

"You try," said the other man as he spurred his horse for the river.

Scott could have easily killed the one who had stayed behind as he struggled to get his wounded brother on the back of his horse. It was a pitiful sight, with the wounded man groaning and babbling out of his head while his brother tried to comfort him. Scott couldn't kill a man outright who was risking his own life to try to save his brother's.

Then three riders came from the shadows and stopped near the outlaw and his fallen brother. There was the sound of a pistol being cocked and Gene's voice telling the outlaw not to move.

Scott sighed and eased his horse ahead. "Boy, am I glad to see you."

They all jerked at the sound of Scott's voice, and he had to yell again to keep from getting shot.

"Where did you come from?" asked Gene.

"I've been here all along."

"You shoot him?" Starky asked, pointing to the wounded one who was now stretched out on the ground below his scared brother.

Scott shook his head. "No, there were three of them to begin with, and I didn't feel like takin' them all on at once. That one on the ground must have gotten shot up by one of you. This one is his brother, and he stopped to help when the other one fell off his horse. The third one ran out on them."

The thief on the ground moved his feet nervously and licked his lips. His hands shook as he held them in the air, and it was hard for him to stand back from his fallen brother on the ground. It didn't look like either of them had reached twenty yet.

"What do you plan on doin' with us?" he asked. "My brother's dyin', I know he is." He started to kneel down.

"Just stay back from him," Gene warned. "And keep those hands up where we can see them."

Starky got down and went to the wounded one. He was getting worse by the second, and from the sound of his coughing and gagging, they were going to be his last seconds. The rain pattered against him and diluted the blood that darkened the back and side of his slicker. In a moment his sounds of agony died down; he let out a long sigh that gurgled in his throat and left him silent.

His brother collapsed over him and shook him, calling his name and pleading for him to come back to life.

"Get up, son," Starky said, helping him from the ground. "Let's go out in the open. We can't help him now."

Starky rounded up the dead thief's horse and put the man over the saddle. They all headed for the edge of the trees while the rain drizzled in the silence and drowned out the low tones of grief from the young outlaw. Janet's face had stayed white the whole time, and it looked like she was fighting to keep her stomach down. For both her and Scott, there had been a lot of killing to get used to in a short while.

The sun greeted them at the edge of the trees. It was starting to work its way through the clouds in the west. The rain was still falling, but it wasn't going to fall much longer, as patches of blue were showing here and there in the sky. On the hillsides, meadowlarks were rejoicing by singing their high, clear songs into the evening sky, and somewhere close by a robin was working on his rain song. The new green shimmered and sparkled as the rays of light picked out the raindrops.

Somehow Scott couldn't enjoy it. In his mind he could see the giant man with the red hair and beard and could hear the outlaw who had been riding with this young thief they now had, telling him to be smart and let his brother die. And the sickness from killing was still with him. It all made a deep, hollow feeling down inside of him, for he knew that if they were ever to see their horses again, this would be only the beginning.

Chapter 6

It was a strange way to meet somebody, looking at him down the bore of a loaded pistol. This young outlaw must feel even more strange than he himself did, Scott thought, for he couldn't know whether he would live to see the sun set again. All he could know for certain was that his brother was dead and that those he once rode with did not care. He was at the mercy of people he had never seen before. Now he stood before them, the tears of mourning still wet on his face, waiting for someone to take a rope from his saddle and throw it over a tree.

"Let's have your name," said Gene.

"Lonnie Taggert," the young thief answered. "That's who I am, and I can't help it." He pointed to the dead one on the horse. "That's my brother, Casey."

"Are you Old Man Taggert's boys?" Gene asked.

He shook his head. "He's our uncle. He took us in when our pa was killed down in Abilene some years back. We owed him, he said, and look what we paid. I guess you're fixin' to hang me."

"Think you deserve it?" Starky asked.

He shrugged. "I was stealin' horses. That's reason enough where I come from."

He didn't care whether he lived or died; for him, everything seemed to be gone. His brother lay draped over a saddle, and everyone else he considered a friend had run off to save their own skins, leaving him and his brother to fend for themselves. It was enough to convince anyone that just about anything else was a better way to make a living than running with a bunch of thieves.

"How many are in with you?" Gene asked.

"I don't know, seven or eight," he answered, keeping his head down.

"What do you mean you don't know?" Gene asked. "Didn't you ride with them?"

He just shrugged.

"Who are they?"

He shrugged again. "I didn't get to know any of them very well."

"Can you beat that?" said Gene, turning to the rest of them. "They leave him and his brother here alone to collect bullet holes, and he's bound to honor."

The kid was silent.

"Didn't you know *any* of them?"

"They're kin," he shouted. "I can't go tellin' on them!"

"Fine kin that'll leave you to die."

"They didn't know," he explained. "I mean, my kin didn't know. I was with a gunman that's in with us. He don't care about nobody."

"You must know his name," Gene said.

The kid shifted back and forth a bit before he spoke. "Rico LaFarge is his name. I don't know any more about him."

Gene looked over at Starky. "That name ring a bell?"

Starky nodded. "He's a tinhorn cutthroat that used

to work with a bunch at the Cimarron crossing. They killed a lot of good cowhands who were just tryin' to make a go of it pushin' beeves up to Kansas."

Scott thought back on the cold voice he had heard telling the kid that he should leave his brother to die.

"Is LaFarge the only one that isn't kin?" Starky asked.

"Yeah, he's the only one."

"So you have just one big family of rustlers," Gene said.

The kid shook his head. "No, we ain't the only ones that've been stealin' stock. We've got lots of help."

"You mean your bunch is tied in with other rustlers?"

The kid nodded. "We're just holdin' up our end of the deal."

"What do you mean by that?" Starky asked.

He lowered his head and started fidgeting around again. "Why should I tell you all this?"

"Do you plan on getting back with them?" Gene asked him.

The boy kicked at a small sagebrush near his boot and thought about how he would answer. He was being careful; maybe he didn't want to die as badly now as he had a short while back.

Finally he looked up at Gene. "They're all the kin I got. It ain't that I agree with how they make a livin', but a man has got to have family just the same."

He had a point. Family is the bigger part of happiness, especially in a big country like this. The hard part was getting him to see that a family like his meant the same thing as having no family. Once a bunch, kin or not, takes to a life of running and killing, it isn't long until they get broken apart. Then being kin won't hold an edge over being strangers; sooner or later, one brother will shoot the other over a few dollars.

"I could've told you that I didn't plan on joinin' back up with them," the kid added, "then took off and found them again. But I didn't think anything I would have to say would keep you from hangin' me if you had a mind to anyway."

"You're right," said Gene. "It wouldn't. You said yourself that a man who'd steal another man's horse deserves to hang."

"Okay, son," Starky came in. "Hanging you right now isn't about to get our horses back for us. I think we all know that. Besides, there's been enough killing around here for one day. Now, you've got to see that your brother gets buried decent, and we've got some horses to find. What do you say we just part company here and now and let it go at that."

The kid studied Starky with a puzzled look. Gene looked over at Starky too but didn't say anything.

"You mean you're ready to let me off scot-free?"

"We haven't got time for that if we want to get on over to those Makoshika badlands and find our horses," Starky said.

The kid's mouth dropped open. "How did you know where we hid out? I didn't think anybody knew."

Starky had a sly grin on his face. "I didn't know until you just now told me."

Gene had a little grin on his face, too. He could have threatened the kid with all sorts of things, and the kid most likely would never have said anything. It took an old hand like Starky and one shrewd statement to get what they wanted to know.

"What made you think of Makoshika?" the kid asked.

"There's not a lot of places big enough to hide that many horses around here and get by with it," Starky said. "Those badlands are harder than hell to get in and out of; a place like that would suit anybody's needs for a horse ranch."

Starky was right. There were a lot of badlands strung out from eastern Montana Territory into the Black Hills and on up through Dakota Territory to the Missouri River. Almost any part of that kind of country would do a pretty good job of hiding men and horses; Starky had just picked out the roughest chunk of it and hoped he had picked right.

"Even if you know they're in Makoshika, you'll never get to them," said the kid, shaking his head.

"What makes you so sure?" Gene asked.

The kid laughed. "I can see you've never been in that country before. My God, if you don't know just where you're goin' you'll be lost forever. It all looks the same."

"We'll manage," said Gene.

The kid laughed again. "No, you won't." He turned to Starky. "You ought to know; you just said the name of that place. Why don't you tell him what it's like in there? He don't believe me."

"What he means, son, is that we'll make the best of it on our own," Starky pointed out. "That is, unless you've got something you'd like to offer on your part."

The kid fidgeted some more and said, "You talked about settin' me free, that right?"

"We talked about not killing you and maybe setting you free," Starky said, "if we could be sure you didn't have any more ideas about stealing stock."

"Like I said, my brother and I got into this thing by way of obligation rather than choice. The way I see things now, I got no brother left and I got no obligation left. Horse thievin' ain't for me."

"Looks like maybe we can help each other," said Starky. "You tell us what we need to know, and we never saw you before."

"That's fair," said the kid. "And you've got to take what I tell you for truth. Some of it you wouldn't believe in a hundred years."

"First we've got to know the story behind these horses," Gene started. "You said there was another bunch of thieves working with you. What do you know about them?"

"There's another bunch from up in the Missouri country in on this thing," the kid said. "A bunch headed up by some guy named Jack Stringer."

Gene turned to Starky. "It seems to me that he's the one the folks in the Judith Basin have been pointing their fingers at for some time now."

Starky nodded. "He and his bunch have been causing trouble clean up into Canada. They hole up in that rough country where the Musselshell hits the Missouri, and nobody's got a prayer of going down in there after them and coming out alive."

"That's the one," the kid said.

"How does he fit into all this down here?" Starky asked.

"Old Man Taggert made a deal to sell some horses to him. He went up a couple of weeks ago and met with Stringer by himself. None of the rest of us know too much about it. The old man don't say much about the business end of it."

"And you all go along with that sort of treatment?" Gene asked.

The kid shrugged. "None of us got anybody else but him."

Gene shook his head. "It's hard to imagine why you and your brother would stick your necks way out like that and risk getting a rope stuck over them and not even know what you're doing it for. Seems to me you both could have just rode on out and said the hell with that kind of thing."

"No, we couldn't," the kid argued. "They'd have killed us if we tried."

"What about LaFarge?" Starky asked. "Does he go along with Old Man Taggert's say-so on things?"

"He gets paid. That's all he cares about."

At the edge of the trees a saddle horse caught their attention. There was no rider anywhere to be seen, and Scott immediately recognized it as belonging to another one of the thieves he had killed earlier.

The kid walked over to where the horse was trying to get the bridle off by rubbing its head against a cottonwood. "That's Ben's horse," he said out loud. "Oh, God, not Ben too!"

"Who's Ben?" Gene called out.

"He's a cousin, younger than me and the only other one near our age. I guess the older ones all got away."

Scott pictured the one he had shot first, putting the bullet into his ribs. The kid would have to be told that his cousin lay dead somewhere near the river, but it wasn't going to be Scott. He didn't want to have to look into any more faces etched with death for a while.

Gene and Starky went back into the trees with the kid. No doubt they'd find both men Scott had killed and maybe somebody else that one of the others had shot. Janet hadn't said one word throughout the whole thing. It wasn't at all like her, and it had Scott concerned. Now that there was just the two of them, he figured it was time to find out what was on her mind.

"Might as well get down and wait for them to get back," he said as he swung his leg over.

Janet didn't say anything but got down and tied her

horse to a nearby tree.

"You sure have been quiet," Scott said. "What's bothering you?"

"I don't feel too good," she answered. "All this killing . . ."

"You knew it would be like this," Scott told her. "At least you should have."

"What about you?" she asked. "Did you kill anybody?"

Scott nodded slowly. "I had to; I was right in among them."

"But they were just boys."

"They were committing a man's crime," Scott said. "It doesn't look like they had much choice from what that kid has been telling us, but this is the way it always seems to work out. It usually ends up that the innocents suffer the most."

"Well, I don't really care what happens from here on, anyway," Janet said.

"Why?" Scott asked quickly.

She was almost in tears when she answered. "I'm afraid Clipper is gone. I think he drowned in the river today."

"Are you sure?"

She nodded. "I'm pretty sure it was him. Gene started shooting, and they pushed a big group of horses over a high bank into the river all at once. They were falling all over each other, and some of them drowned."

"What makes you so sure Clipper was one of them?" Scott asked. "Clipper's not the only palomino in the country, you know."

"But he was in this bunch," Janet argued. "And you heard the kid tell us they were horse thieves. Oh, I wish Gene could have gotten him out."

"Gene went into the river after him?"

Janet nodded, the tears forming heavily in her eyes. "Gene went in to try and rope him, but we couldn't find him again. I know he feels bad because he thinks it's his fault from shooting at the thieves. But he's gone, now. Clipper's gone." She turned away and went off by herself.

"I don't think you should give up hope just yet," Scott called after her. "Sure, the horses were stolen, but I didn't see any Circle 6 stock at all."

She turned around and said, "You mean you didn't see any of our stock either? Gene and Starky both said the same thing."

"I saw a couple or three head of SH horses," Scott went on. "And there was a lot of Sugar Bowl stock, but I didn't see anything of ours."

Janet took a deep breath. "It looked so much like him, so big and beautiful."

"But you didn't see a brand to be sure, did you?"

"No. We were on the wrong side for Circle 6, and his left side wasn't branded. That's why I'm almost sure it was him."

There was no way Scott could assure her that it wasn't her horse she had seen drown in the Powder River. It was hard to tell how many horses had crossed before they had gotten there and whether any of them had been Circle 6 stock. It was anybody's guess where Janet's horse was at the moment, alive or dead.

"Tomorrow I'd like to take a ride down the river a ways and see if I can find any of those horses," she said. "I'd really like to find him."

Scott didn't know what to say to her. Whether her horse had drowned or not, searching the river wasn't the answer. She wouldn't be happy if she found him dead, and she wouldn't be happy if she didn't find him at all; those would be her only two choices. Finding him alive wasn't in the cards right then. The thieves had everything that had gotten across the river with them, and the few on this side were already bunched up on the hilltops, grazing. They already knew there were no Circle 6 horses on their side of the river.

"I don't think you should search the river," Scott said. "But whether Clipper was in that bunch or not, Gene risked his life to help you. I hope you appreciate it."

She nodded. "I thanked him already. I can't understand why he did it, though. I didn't think he even liked me."

"Gene hasn't been saying much about anything lately," said Scott, "but I can tell by the way he looks at you, he'd like to talk more."

Scott hoped what he had said would cheer her up, for he knew she had developed something for Gene also. He had seen this the first day at the JO line cabin. But now Janet had only her horse on her mind and cared about little else. Scott hoped that what he had told her earlier about thinking there were no Circle 6 horses in this bunch would prove to be true. If not, it would take Janet a long time to recover, and it could mean losing the Circle 6.

Chapter 7

While Gene and Starky looked through the trees along the river for more horses and dead thieves, Scott and Janet talked more about Clipper and the other Circle 6 horses. There was a good chance their horses had not been in this bunch. The question was, Where were they?

The badlands were every bit as wild and rugged as the kid had said. The Plains Indian tribes from the Missouri River down into the Black Hills were deathly afraid of the place and gave it a wide berth. The Sioux called it *Makoshika*, which meant something about bad ground and evil spirits. The name had gotten passed around the country pretty fast, and each time another story went with it. Since the area was so rugged, travelers went around it rather than waste time trying to cross. It was a good place to hide out in. To hear the bullwhackers and buffalo hunters tell it, the Sioux had come up with a pretty good name for the place.

As Scott and Janet talked more, they both came to the realization that the worst going lay still ahead and that it was going to take a lot of fortitude to stick it out.

Gene and Starky came out of the trees, followed closely by the kid. He was leading three more horses with bodies draped across them. The clouds had all lifted by now, and the sun was reaching for the horizon, bathing the loose horses on the slopes in a reddish glow. Overhead the sky was taking on a dark tone that promised nightfall before too long.

The kid said, "I think I'll try and find a place in among these trees to bury my kin. I'd be obliged if you folks didn't let it get out to anyone else. I'll leave them unmarked, and that way they'll rest in peace without some lawman diggin' them up for some reason."

"We got no reason to say a thing to nobody," said Starky.

"Guess you'll be takin' them horses back directly then," the kid stated.

"Those horses don't belong to any of us," Starky told him. "I reckon they'll get back to their rightful owners in time."

The kid gave Starky a puzzled look.

"No, they don't belong to any of us," Starky repeated. "We're after Circle 6 stock."

"Hell, we were workin' too far south to pick up any Circle 6 horses. Old Man Taggert himself must have stolen your stock."

"You mean Old Man Taggert isn't leading your bunch?" Starky asked.

"He sent us farther south with Bull, his oldest son," the kid explained. "And then he decided to send the gunman, LaFarge, along in case we needed a good gun. Bull would rather crush a man than shoot him."

Scott remembered the huge redheaded man he had seen along the river earlier who had been waving at the other thieves from the opposite shore. Scott had never seen another human being that big before. There was no doubt somebody that size could easily kill a man with his bare hands.

"Old Man Taggert and the rest of the bunch must have your horses, then," the kid went on. "He most likely crossed sometime before noon."

"Why weren't you all together?" Gene asked.

"The old man figured we could get more horses workin' in two separate groups," the kid answered. "We were supposed to cross with the horses we ended up with and meet up with the old man tonight at the head of O'Fallon Creek farther east. I remember because he told us not to be longer than three days, and Bull was cuttin' notches in a little piece of wood he had in his pocket to keep track of the days."

"They'll be late getting up there," Starky put in. "And there can't be many men or horses left after today."

"I'll bet the old man's ready to skin somebody alive," the kid said. "I'm glad I'm not gettin' ready to face him. Even Bull gets plumb scared when he blows up."

"Judging by the number of these he leaves behind, he must blow up a lot," said Gene, holding up the empty .50-caliber Sharps cartridge he had picked up back at the ranch.

The kid nodded. "If that is painted red, it's his. He uses that as his trademark. He leaves one with everybody he works with."

"Do you suppose he gave one to Jack Stringer?" Starky asked.

"I would imagine," the kid answered, pulling a cartridge of his own from a pants pocket. He handed it to Starky. "Here, I won't have any need for this now."

Starky took it from him. "After you got to the head of O'Fallon Creek, what was supposed to happen then?"

"We were supposed to take them on over to

Makoshika together from there," said the kid. "That's where Jack Stringer comes in."

Starky juggled the empty shell. "Is he going in there to get the horses?"

The kid shuffled his feet uncomfortably. "Like I said, Old Man Taggert don't like to say much about his deals. I guess he thinks the less we know, the better it is for him. But I heard him tellin' Bull the other night that Stringer was supposed to come down into Makoshika to get the horses this time. This will be the first time Stringer has ever been down there. They usually deal at an old line cabin up on the Musselshell River, but I guess people were starting to wonder about it some."

Now it seemed as if things were starting to come together. Both Old Man Taggert and Jack Stringer were starting to feel the squeeze of an angry public, and they were beginning to arrange their dealings so that they would never be meeting at the same place steadily. That made it harder for anyone to pinpoint one place where they could catch a bunch of thieves with horses.

"I know Bull and LaFarge are supposed to meet them to lead them into the horse ranch," the kid went on. "Stringer must want those horses bad to come clear down here."

Starky was still juggling the shell. "Do you know where Bull and LaFarge were supposed to meet Stringer and his bunch?"

The kid got a positive look on his face. "I didn't hear anyone say for sure, but I've got a real good idea. There's an old wood yard at the mouth of Box Elder Creek down the Yellowstone a ways. It's the biggest rathole you ever laid eyes on."

"What's so bad about the place?" Gene asked.

"It's just a bunch of old cabins that have just sat

there and rotted since the end of the steamboat days,''
the kid explained. ''An old hag named Crazy Alice and
her son live up there.''

''Crazy Alice?'' said Gene.

''Yeah, Crazy Alice. You could see why they call
her that if you ever saw her. She's pretty well known by
all the thieves in this part of the country. She's turned
one of the cabins up there into a saloon, and she runs
some girls on the side in one of the other shacks, her
and her son, Scully. The place is filthy, and all the
people up there are filthy. It makes my skin crawl to
talk about it.''

''How far is it from here?'' Starky asked.

''It's a full day's ride. I've been up there once, and
that was enough. I don't even care to remember it.''

''When is this deal supposed to come off?'' Gene
asked.

''Within the week, close as I can tell,'' the kid
answered. ''All I know is that Stringer wants to buy
about thirty head of good horses from the old man.''

''You're pretty sure about this wood yard?'' Gene
asked.

''I'd say so. In fact, there's a better than even chance
somebody will be up there tomorrow. Bull and
LaFarge spend a lot of time up there. I know that's
where they'll be just as soon as they get the stolen
horses into the horse ranch in Makoshika. They don't
help with changin' the brands, and they'd both rather
spend their money drinkin' and whorin' up there than
any other place.''

Starky stuck the rifle shell he had been juggling into
his pocket. ''It looks like our move now.''

''Well, I don't want to have any more to do with
this,'' the kid said. ''I've lost too much as it is.''

''You won't have to worry about losing any more,''

Starky told him. "Most likely the rest of them think you're dead now. You can get yourself a new start with some cow outfit in another part of the country and forget you were ever a part of all this."

"I wish I could," the kid said. "Maybe I'll head over west into the Gallatin country. I've heard that's a real pretty place."

"It is," said Starky, holding out his hand. "That's a good place to get started over, and we all wish you luck."

"I'm beholden to you all for choosin' not to hang me," the kid said. "I won't ever take nothin' that ain't mine ever again. It don't pay, it don't pay at all. I lost my whole family on account of it." He took a deep breath and kept his eyes on the stolen horses that had escaped, now grazing peacefully out away from the river. "People ain't supposed to do to one another what the old man done to us. Someday he'll be sorry for it. Some day."

The kid left, leading the horses with his fallen brother and cousins laid across them. It would be a dark and lonely night for him. Scott watched him a few extra moments and then turned his horse toward the river with the others.

They loosened the cinches on their saddles a notch to make it easier for the horses to swim, and then they forced them out into the river. It took some firm persuasion to get them into the water as they weren't eager to fight the heavy current that pounded against their sides and sucked hard at their legs from underneath. It was easy to hear their labored breathing even over the rush of the river.

Scott was straining with all his might to hold on as his buckskin fought the current. He was holding his guns and bedroll over his head with one hand and gripping the reins and the horse's mane with the other. It was a grueling test of endurance that drained his strength.

His buckskin struggled out of the river onto the other shore and stood wheezing with exhaustion. Fatigued himself, Scott slid down from the saddle and dropped his arms as a dull numbness crept into them. His ears were ringing with the roar of the water, and the blood was pounding in his skull, but he heard yelling. He fought the throbbing in his arms and squinted into the sunset to look for the others.

Then it seemed the whole world was yelling right next to him. Beside him was Gene, shouting and pointing into the current while Starky stumbled in his water-soaked clothing to get up alongside. Scott followed Gene's arm out into the river, and his heart came up into his mouth.

Janet's horse had stopped on a sandbar near the middle of the river and was lunging around in a panic. Her saddle was tilted off to one side, and she was clawing at the horse's mane, trying to raise herself straight above the horse's back and get her feet out of the stirrups.

Gene came back from his horse with a rope and shook the water from it while Starky and Scott yelled for her to hang on. Scott forgot the pain in his arms and was trying to think of the best thing to do. Scott watched Gene with the rope; it seemed the only chance to save her.

Gene let the loop fly. It was a long toss that sailed way over Janet and the horse, falling uselessly into the river and washing down with the flow. Gene cursed loudly and pulled the lariat back for another try. This time the loop fell just behind her and the rope came up over the horse's rump. The strange feel of it spooked

the horse into a wild lunge; Janet didn't have time to
yell before she hit the river with a dull slosh.

Scott's belly tightened as if he'd been squeezed in a
huge vise. Starky made a throaty yell, and Gene ran out
into the current as if he were going to catch her.

The water took Janet so fast that they didn't even see
her until she had grabbed on to the branches of a small
cottonwood that was lodged on another sandbar
downstream. They all ran down the bank, fighting their
way through the tangles of brush. The lower half of
Scott's body tingled with the wet sting of rose and
gooseberry as their sharp-thorned branches slapped
against him. He spooked Janet's horse where it stood
wheezing on the bank with the saddle hanging awk-
wardly under its belly.

Gene said, "I'm going out after her!"

"Take your horse," Starky advised him.

Gene was tying one end of a rope around his middle.
"I can't risk it with a horse," he said. "I'll just swim
out with this rope around me and take another one for
her. You two will just have to see if you can pull us
in."

He gave Scott and Starky the other end of his rope
and lunged into the river. He had started far enough
upstream that he figured the current wouldn't take him
past her. If he misjudged either the distance to her or
his swimming ability, he wouldn't get a second
chance.

Starky took a turn around a nearby tree trunk, and
both he and Scott held the rope firmly and shouted out
to Janet while Gene worked his way out to her. She had
to be holding on to that small cottonwood with only the
sheer will to live by now. The water was tearing at her
without mercy, and she was struggling with all she had
to keep her grip on the slick branches. She even had her

legs clamped around and through them as she tried to climb out of the current, but her weight was always too much for the young tree; the limber branches bent in an arc as she dipped in and out of the water. It looked like she was going to use all her strength and fall back one of those times and never come up. But then Gene got there.

Scott swallowed hard to keep his throat open as he watched them. They were both dog-tired, and their movements showed it. After what seemed forever, Gene got the other rope over Janet and took the loop in tight under her arms. Then he put a few turns of the loose end around himself and got ready to head back for shore. Scott knew that they wouldn't make it by themselves.

"I'm going out there and help them," he yelled to Starky, and started into the river with a quick rush.

The river was no longer roaring, nor was Scott's heart hammering to get out of his body as it had before. Only a fierce determination held him, a wild desire to forge his way out into that churning broth of moving water and overcome it to save the lives of those two people. His body seemed immune to the icy cold of the water, and his hands gripped the rope strong and firm as he pulled and swam his way toward them. *You can't have them! You can't have them!* He told it to the river over and over in his mind, and finally he got himself out to where they were struggling and coughing in the brown gurgling froth that boiled among the branches of the small cottonwood.

Their eyes were glazed with exhaustion, and their breath came in hoarse rasps. He yelled at them and sparked a new determination in them with his voice and strong grip. Soon Gene was holding on to him and Janet to Gene as they started back toward the shoreline.

Starky yelled out to them, and Scott could feel the
strength of ten men pulling them as he saw that the rope
was wrapped around the saddlehorn of his buckskin.
They were moving fast and steadily. If only Gene and
Janet could hold on until they got there.

Their feet touched sand, and they all gasped and
yelled and cheered at the same time. In the red twilight,
Starky was above them, dragging with strong hands,
sweat dripping from his brow.

Scott sank to his knees while his whole body shook.
Starky and Gene had Janet on her feet, half walking,
half carrying her so that she wouldn't pass out. She was
trying to talk and breath at the same time she choked up
river water and gagged.

Behind them the river pounded and roared while the
sun made a calm and peaceful descent over the western
horizon. Little birds were darting back and forth from
the cover of the trees, taking advantage of the change in
the weather and chasing each other in their nesting
flights. The slopes across the river were pitch black
now, and Scott was sure the young thief had probably
finished burying his relatives a long time ago and was
well on his way west, never knowing how close to
death the people who had chosen not to hang him had
come.

Chapter 8

The night was still and peaceful. Overhead, stars shot through the entire length of the sky. The round moon, still nearly full, spread a soft light across the valley.

Breaking the gentle night was the surging rush of the Powder River, roaring at the top of its banks and pounding its way down the valley toward the Yellowstone. It had nearly stopped their chase after the horses.

Scott sat gazing into the flickering light of the fire, trying to fight the idea that any hope of finding their horses was gone. They had lost a lot of precious time fighting the Powder River, and it had played the horses out too much for them to think of going any farther that night. It was late, and everyone should have been asleep long ago; but the nervous energy was still there, and no one felt much like turning in. The air was getting warmer as time went on, and that was the only thing that helped the otherwise cheerless atmosphere. Scott thought back on something Starky had said about being lucky to be alive and wondered why they weren't all dancing.

Janet was near the fire, pouring canteen water over her head and doing her best to comb the river water out

of her hair. She was wearing some extra things Gene
had brought with him until her own dried out. They
hung baggy and funny on her, but no one seemed to
notice. Gene came over and sat down beside her,
fidgeting with a small piece of kindling wood.

"I just about got you killed," he said to her. "I sure
am sorry about that."

Janet grabbed an old cloth and began to dry her hair.
She looked up at Gene and said, "You don't have
anything to be sorry about. If it hadn't been for you, I
probably *would* be dead."

"Your horse wouldn't have thrown you, though, if I
wasn't so bad with a rope," Gene said, breaking little
pieces of kindling as he spoke.

"I couldn't have stayed on, anyway. My saddle was
slipping, and that fool horse was crazy. There's no
need for you to take off your coat of shining armor."

Gene looked up at her from his kindling, and a little
smile appeared on his lips. Janet responded with a
smile of her own, and Scott decided it would be a good
time to curry the sand and mud out of his horse's coat.

Starky showed up in a matter of seconds and said,
"That's a good idea. I think I'll rub my horse
down, too."

Scott and Starky got busy on their horses, and there
was a short period of silence before Starky said,
"You're being pretty quiet tonight, Scott. Something
the matter?"

"Oh, I'm having a hard time convincing myself that
our luck hasn't run out on us. I can't see how we'll ever
catch up with our horses now, not after this thing with
the river. Maybe I'd do more good back at the ranch
with Pa."

"We've come this far," Starky pointed out. "No
sense in crossing that river again now that we've licked
it once."

"We're still a far cry from our horses," said Scott. "I don't know that I understand all this. I'm not even sure now who has our stock."

"My guess is Old Man Taggert still has them and that he's headed for Makoshika with them," Starky said. "I know he works that country and knows it pretty well. The odds are better than even we'll trail him into that country. Just so we get there before his trade deal falls into place."

"That's what I don't understand," said Scott. "What is all this trading back and forth between Taggert and this Jack Stringer from the Missouri?"

"It's good business," Starky explained. "Both gangs steal horses from different parts of the country and then swap the stolen stock so those who go looking for them will get confused. Don't let it bother you, though. We'll catch up with them."

"They've got a big jump on us. And I know we've got to rest these horses up good so they can get their strength back. I just feel so helpless."

Starky nodded. "I don't blame you, Scott. But we can't give up on those horses yet, not when we've got good ground for tracking. This mud will make it easy."

"We really shouldn't have any trouble finding their tracks," Scott said, perking up a bit.

"And we'll be able to move a lot faster than them, being they've got horses to drive," Starky added. "All of us can keep up a good pace, I can see that. Especially Janet; she'd probably be the last one to quit."

Scott laughed. "That's a fact."

"You don't usually see a woman out chasing horse thieves," Starky commented. "But after being around Janet for a while, nothing she would do would surprise me."

"You got it," Scott said. "She doesn't do things

like any other woman would. I guess you already figured that from when she pulled the saddle gun on you back in the hills yesterday."

Starky came around the front of Scott's horse and stopped beside him. "You know, that's the first time I've ever had anyone do that to me, man or woman. It took a lot of guts to do that."

"She's got plenty of those," Scott said. "And you know how bad she wants that horse of hers back."

"I never knew a horse to mean that much to someone before."

"I don't know if it's the horse as much as her just not getting any satisfaction out of people." Scott stopped to clean the loose horsehair out of his currycomb. "She's had a few rough times when somebody or another let her down. I guess she figures there's more future in loving a horse than a person. At least the horse has never let her down."

"Well, she sure is determined," Starky said with a little nod of his head. "She won't let anything stand in her way."

"As near as I can tell about Gene, he seems to be a lot like Janet," Scott surmised.

Starky went over to his own horse and got back to work on it. "I don't know much about Gene's background," he said, "but he don't have any trouble handling a gun. I saw that at the river. He can do more than just break horses."

"I felt the same way," said Scott. "He made short work of that outlaw in the barn back at the C Bar S. But I don't think he's an outlaw himself. He's been too good to me and Janet. It's not everybody who'll go out in the middle of a high river for somebody they just met, whether they're as pretty as Janet or not—and twice in one day at that!"

"Twice?" Starky said.

"He went out during the fight this afternoon for a horse Janet thought was Clipper. It went under with a bunch of other horses on top of it, though, and he couldn't get a rope in among them all. From what Janet says, the horse ended up on the bottom with a few others."

"She knows now that it wasn't her horse, though, doesn't she?"

"Yeah, she heard that kid say Old Man Taggert has our stock. But I still don't know what kind of chance we got to find them." Scott moved his currycomb through the buckskin's coat; his feeling of dejection and hopelessness was starting to come back. "I think they've got us beat now that they're way past the river. You know, it's not that far to Makoshika from here, and they'll no doubt have the brands changed way before we've got a chance to get them back."

Starky came back to where Scott was working, pulling horsehair out of his own currycomb as he walked. He got next to Scott and traced his finger around the brand on the buckskin's shoulder.

"You know," he said, "I think they've got one big problem with your horses, though. A Circle 6 ain't the easiest brand in the world to change." He started rubbing his chin and turned to Scott. "What would they change it to? If that 6 wasn't in the middle of that circle like that, things would be easier for them."

"How do you mean?" Scott asked, stopping his work to listen.

"Well, they can't change the 6 too easy, since the inside curve of the letter comes back to almost a full circle." He ran his finger around the mark to show Scott. "Whoever designed that brand wasn't born yesterday. See, now, no one can make that into an 8, or anything else for that matter, without leaving one hell of a mess for a brand. And since the circle is so big that it covers damn near the whole shoulder, nobody can stick another number or letter next to it and still keep it on the shoulder. See what I mean?''

Scott thought about it a moment. All of a sudden he had new hope; Starky's point was a good one. If the thieves tried to add any more to the Circle 6 shoulder brand, they would end up having to move off onto the ribs. That would never do. And the Circle 6 horses all had fresh brands from this spring, hardly two weeks ago. They could add another brand to one of the hips or to the other shoulder, but two fresh brands on one animal would make a buyer ask a lot of questions.

"I think you're right," said Scott, moving his buckskin more in line with the firelight to study the brand. "What do you think they'll do about that?''

"Some of them can do a lot with a pair of tweezers,'' Starky said. "But that takes a real good man and a lot of time. The way I see it, even if they've got a man who can touch brands up like that, they haven't got the time to work them all over and do it right—not before Stringer is supposed to come down for them, anyway.''

"How will that help us?'' Scott asked.

"I've been working up a plan that just might get those horses back for us,'' Starky said. "From what the kid told us, Bull and LaFarge will most likely show up at the wood yard after they get the horses into Makoshika. That should be sometime late tomorrow afternoon. That means Bull and LaFarge will most likely be ready to hightail it down out of those badlands to that wood yard by the day after tomorrow, after the horses are settled and they've convinced Old Man Taggert that everything is safe enough so they can leave. Right?''

Scott nodded. "So what are you getting at?''

"How would you like to be part of Jack Stringer's bunch?" Starky said with a grin. "We'll go up to that wood yard and just have Bull and LaFarge lead us right up into Makoshika to those horses."

"What?"

"The way I see it," Starky explained, still grinning, "we could set ourselves up to be part of Stringer's gang of thieves if we were to get to that wood yard ahead of anybody else. We can tell Bull and LaFarge that we're part of his bunch that just never got over this far east before."

Scott frowned. "They're bound to wonder why Stringer himself didn't come along. I don't see how we could make a scheme like that work."

"I think I've got that figured," Starky said. "We can tell them that Stringer is holed up until the stockmen in the country cool off about this rustling thing. After what we did to them earlier today, they'll surely believe there's some mad cowboys running loose. We can convince them that folks know about Stringer and that he wants to avoid getting his neck stretched if at all possible. I think Bull and LaFarge could see that reasoning plain enough."

"That's going to be a tricky plan to pull off," Scott said, still skeptical. "How can you be sure they'll buy our story about being part of Stringer's gang? Janet being along won't make it any easier."

Starky smiled and reached into his pocket. "Remember what that kid gave me just before he left tonight?" He held up the empty .50 Sharps casing. "No doubt Old Man Taggert gave a few of these out to Stringer's bunch, since the kid said he gives them to folks he does business with. And since most people don't mark their shells with red paint, Bull and LaFarge will most likely swallow our story. As for

Janet, I don't think she'll have any trouble proving she's rough enough to run with horse thieves, especially if one of them makes her mad. What do you think?''

"I'll have to agree with you about Janet," Scott said with a little laugh. "Janet could run with any bunch of toughs she chose to and get along fine. Just fine.''

"The only thing we've got to do is talk Gene into it," Starky said. "I don't know if he'll want to go to playacting at all. He's used to doing things pretty straightforward.''

Scott continued thinking. "I'm having a hard time getting any confidence in it myself, but I haven't come up with anything better. My worry is convincing Bull and LaFarge that we're part of Stringer's bunch.''

Starky moved to where Scott could see his eyes. "Ninety percent of it is right up here," he said, putting a finger to his forehead. "You've got to make them believe what you want them to believe. You've got to assure them that you would just as soon kill them as do business with them; that's how men of that sort live. I can make you think right now that I'm just about ready to shoot you down where you stand.''

"I believe you're right," said Scott, shrinking back from his stare.

"Eat nails, boy," Starky said jokingly, clapping him on the back. "Before we're through, Bull and LaFarge will think we're just about the meanest bunch of bastards that ever set a running iron to stolen horse-flesh.''

They went back into the light of the fire and talked with Gene and Janet about the plan. Gene frowned now and again while Starky spelled out what they would do. It did seem like a wild idea at first, but as he did with Scott, Starky put it together in such a fashion that there seemed to be some merit. Any way they looked at it, they would have to have a lot of luck and good timing to make it work. But they all realized that there wasn't going to be any easy way to go about getting their horses back.

Scott laid his bedroll out and crawled inside. It was still a little damp in places from the river crossing, but he was bone-tired by now, and just the feel of something soft worked at his eyelids Still, that little bit of dampness was there and it slowly crept into him, especially when he thought of what could happen if they got in with those horse thieves and something went wrong.

Chapter 9

They were in the saddle and gone as soon as it was light enough to see. The trail the thieves had left was broad and easy to follow. They reached the head of O'Fallon Creek early in the day, and the trail showed where Bull and LaFarge's bunch had met up with Old Man Taggert's group; they had headed due east in a big hurry. No doubt their course would be a straight shot to the horse ranch in Makoshika.

It was cause for celebration in a way. They knew right where their horses were going and had a fairly good plan devised for getting to them. Now all that mattered was being able to stay alive in the process.

Just after midday the country broke up into some of the most rugged stretches of ground God ever made. The hills had turned from rolling grass to open stands of scrag timber and sagebrush. Big mounds of bare earth poked up in the bottoms and at the heads of the gullies, while patches of hard-pan clay splotched the drainages and bleached out white where the salts had crusted on the surface of the ground. They were getting closer to the hellhole the Sioux called *Makoshika*.

The deeper they rode into that country, the worse it got. The drainages got steeper, and the ground got more barren. It was a lot slower going, and the trail was getting harder to follow. The sun was coming down as strong now as it had all year, bringing summer to mind. Another reminder of warm weather came to them in the form of a small flock of turkey vultures circling slowly over something on the other side of the next ridge.

From the top of the ridge, they could see a dead horse lying in the bottom of a gully along the trail below. They rode down, and a half dozen magpies stopped their pecking and flew noisily off the top of the carcass.

"My God, it's one of our horses," Scott exclaimed as he got down from his buckskin for a closer look. "That's Pa's horse. Oh, my God!" It was a pretty roan that had died in the prime of life.

"Looks like he's been ridden to death," said Starky. "I doubt if they even changed horses after crossin' the river. They most likely just kept pushin' them as fast as they could."

The horse showed signs of having died under a lot of exertion. The hair was matted from sweat that had turned to a heavy lather, and the marks from the latigo strap on the saddle were plain around its middle.

"What kind of a man would do that to a horse?" Scott asked through gritted teeth.

"Those horses are just merchandise to them," Starky said. "From the looks of things, they don't know how to take care of their merchandise. I'm afraid this is only the first one that we'll find."

There were others. Soon they found two more dead horses, both from other outfits. Aside from the pain she felt for those they found, a look of dreadful worry etched itself into Janet's face. Would they find her palomino in the same condition? What would she do if they found her beautiful horse lying in the bottom of

some godforsaken gulch with his life spent at the hands
of a bunch of merciless killers? Scott talked to her
about it; Gene and Starky both put in a few words. Her
face still kept that frightened look.

The last horse they found lay only moments from
death. It had been abandoned to die at the bottom of a
large gully. There was a Circle 6 brand on the left
shoulder, and both Scott and Janet recognized it as a
two-year-old mare that had been one of their prize
horses.

"Hardly more than a colt," Scott said sadly. "And
so pretty."

It lay on its side, unblinking and barely breathing.
The young horse tried to raise its head but did not have
the strength. Janet broke into tears and unleashed a
flurry of angry words as Gene put the animal out of its
misery.

"We can't be far from their horse ranch now," said
Starky. "If they push this hard much further, they'll
lose all of them."

"They don't care how many they lose," said Gene.
"Their big kick is in stealing them."

Scott shook his head. "I just don't know how people
can do it."

"I'm going to do my share of the shooting from now
on," Janet promised. "I'm through feeling sorry for
any of them!"

"You can't let this affect your thinking when we
start trying to get our horses back," Starky told her.
"We all feel the same, but we've got to keep our heads
unless we want to die the same way."

Farther on, the trail hit a good-sized drainage. Scott
knew it to be Cedar Creek. The tracks didn't cross it but
turned and followed it north instead. It was hard to
understand why the thieves had chosen to head north

instead of crossing the creek and continuing east. A few miles down the creek, they got their answer.

Scott held them up as he caught sight of a small cabin nestled close to the bank farther down. A lone man was pushing a plow behind a mule in harness in a nearby field.

"Can't say as I remember him being here last time I was through," Scott commented.

"He's most likely new in the country," Starky said. "There's been some families like that drifting into the country right along lately."

"That trail goes right down there to his cabin," Gene said, pointing to the wide swath of hoofprints in the ground. "Maybe he had some stock they figured on making off with."

Starky nodded. "You're most likely right there, Gene. That being the case, we'd best go down slow and easy and stay in the open where he can see us. He'll for sure wonder what we're doing way out here."

They moved down through the still air of the afternoon. The sound of their approach carried down to the field, and the man behind the plow stopped his work and stared. As Starky had predicted, the sight of four strangers riding out of nowhere threw him into a panic. He made for the cabin at a dead run. In a moment, he was at the door with a shotgun.

"He can't reach too far with that scattergun," said Gene. "Let's move in a ways."

"Hold back a minute," Starky advised him. "We could move a hell of a lot farther in, and he still couldn't touch us. But let's not scare him."

"Get out of here," came a shout from the cabin doorway. "We ain't got nothin' left. You're wastin' your time if you think we got any horses."

"We're looking for some of our own," Starky

yelled. "We're not here to rob you."

"I said get out!"

"We'll come in with our hands up. We just want to talk."

The homesteader stopped and thought it over for a moment. "Come on ahead," he yelled out. "Just keep your hands up, though." He stepped out of his cabin with the shotgun leveled.

They came up near the cabin with their hands out where the homesteader could see them. He seemed to ease up when he saw Janet.

"Long way from anywhere for a woman," he said.

"I'm after my horse," she told him. "I don't care where I have to go to find him."

The homesteader lowered the shotgun and nodded. He turned his head back in the doorway and said, "It's safe to come on out. These folks ain't no rustlers."

A woman appeared in the doorway and moved out to join her husband. She was flanked by a young woman who appeared to be close to Janet's age. Her eyes were the same blue as Janet's, but her hair was as dark as Janet's was light. She, too, was a pretty woman.

"This is our fourth day after a gang of thieves," said Starky. "We followed their trail to your place here."

The homesteader got an aggravated look on his face and made a motion behind himself with the barrel of the shotgun. "I've got an empty corral because of them. They came through early this mornin' and stopped just long enough to take our three saddle horses and kill the milk cow. It looked like they were in one hell of a hurry, which I figure was lucky for us." He looked at his wife and daughter with a feeling of thankfulness. "No tellin' if we'd be alive now, otherwise."

"We ran into them back at the Powder River," Gene

said. "We got about half of them, and the rest know we're on their trail."

The homesteader's daughter moved her eyes from Janet to Starky to Scott and then settled her gaze on Gene.

"Are you a lawman?" she asked.

"Sort of," Gene answered.

She nodded and gave him an admiring smile.

"They went east from here," the homesteader informed them. "My guess is that they're holed up over there in them badlands somewhere."

"We heard there's a big group of them in there," Starky said. "That's where we're headed now."

The homesteader shook his head. "I wouldn't go into that country over there for love nor money. There's too many men that have, and they ain't come out to this day."

"Well, we're about to take this opportunity to check those stories out," Gene said with confidence.

The homesteader studied Gene a moment. "Yeah, I don't doubt that you've got as good a chance as anybody. While you're in there, keep an eye pealed for a Lazy J on the right hip."

They bade the homesteader and his family good-bye and crossed Cedar Creek behind the cabin. The trail wound into the east, and they stayed on it, keeping an eye out for signs of anything suspicious ahead. As they rode, Scott gave Starky the lead and dropped back to visit with Gene. In a moment, Janet had also pulled her horse alongside Gene.

"Why didn't you just stay back there with that sodbuster's daughter?" she said to him. "I thought for sure you would."

Gene looked puzzled. "What? I don't know what you're talking about."

"Oh, no, I don't suppose you do," Janet retorted. "You just had to stare, didn't you?"

Gene looked at her and shook his head. "She wasn't that interesting."

"You couldn't prove that by the way you acted," she said.

Scott laughed a little. "Why, Janet, you're not jealous, are you?"

"Shut up, Scott," she said, and spurred her horse ahead to join Starky.

They were just coming into the Sand Creek drainage. They were at the back door to Makoshika now, and they were going to have to make a decision about what they wanted to do.

"This is it," Starky said. "We're looking into the country where those thieves have their horse ranch. We can either take our chances going after them now or stick to the original plan of trying the wood yard on Box Elder Creek first."

"God, that's a rough-looking son of a bitch in there," Gene said half under his breath as he looked into the broken landscape ahead of them. "Good place to get bushwhacked."

Starky nodded in agreement. "That's the biggest concern we'd have going in there," he said. "Right now they're expecting us to just follow this trail they left. It's a cinch they'll be waiting for us."

Gene rubbed his brow. "That wood yard thing looks to be the best idea we've got right now. At least it's better than a sure chance of getting shot up if we go into Makoshika."

Starky peered into the sun. "We've got a solid four hours of daylight left. We could go on down the creek here into Glendive for supplies and be halfway up to that wood yard before the sun even starts going down.

If Crazy Alice and her girls are as popular with Bull and the other thieves as that kid seemed to think, we ought to be able to run into some of them up there easy. Once we convince them we're part of Stringer's bunch, they'll lead us right to the stock.''

''What if we can't convince them we're part of Stringer's bunch?'' Janet asked.

Starky looked at her a moment. ''Then horses will be the least of our worries.''

They got their supplies and moved north of Glendive to a little creek named for the town. It was a good place to camp, and the wood yard was only a leisurely morning's ride farther on. By that time, some of Taggert's men should be headed for Crazy Alice's.

They got the horses rubbed down and picketed; it would be a good chance to let them catch up on their eating and get back some of the strength that had been pounded out of them during the chase. From here on the going would be even rougher, and they couldn't be expected to perform if they weren't kept in good shape. They had just seen the results of running horses to death, and it stuck in their minds.

Glendive Creek was running clean now that the storm was over two days past. The air had stayed warm, and there was still a little time left before dark, and so they decided to make use of the clear running water. Baths and laundry were the order of the day.

Scott found Starky up the creek from camp, throwing a fishline tied to a willow into the current. He lowered himself onto the bank next to Starky.

''Thought I'd get us a mess of fish for supper,'' said Starky.

''That's pretty stout line,'' Scott commented. ''You must think there's some real lunkers in here.''

"I'm used to the big ones up on the Missouri," Starky said with a wink. He pulled up a flopping trout that had grabbed his hook. "But these little fellas are tasty, just the same."

"Little fella?" Scott said with a laugh. "That's a two-pounder at least."

Starky laughed. "Just a little fella."

Scott looked around and asked, "Where's Gene and Janet?"

Starky pointed up the creek. "There's a nice big hole up around that bend. 'I'd be up there fishin' now if it weren't for them two. It just ain't fair."

"What do you mean?"

"I mean it ain't fair they should be takin' a bath in the best fishin' hole in these parts."

Scott blushed. "You mean they're both up there?"

Starky nodded with a grin. "I guess that's what warm spring evenings are for. Just the same, I wish they would have left that fishin' hole for me."

Chapter 10

The wood yard at the mouth of Box Elder Creek wasn't any more than a few old buildings slumping with age and neglect, perched on a small flat where the creek flowed into the Yellowstone River. It was easy to see that the weather was getting the best of the buildings, and clusters of weeds in between them were starting to take good size in the warm sunshine. It had been a number of years since the last steamboat had stopped on its trip upriver to take on wood here. Now that the steamboats were a thing of the past, the wood yards were all vacant and nobody paid much attention to them. Places like that in the middle of nowhere were good for the horse-stealing business.

"This is it," Starky informed them. "Put on your best horse thief face."

"I'm ready," said Janet. "That's for damn sure."

"You'll let us handle it, though," Gene told her. "There may be some shooting."

"I figure you'll need some help before it's over," she said matter of factly, readjusting her hat over her pretty hair. "I'll let you handle it, but I'll get my licks in. Nobody steals a horse from me that I spent eight years of my life training and caring for and gets away

with it.'' Her deep blue eyes were flashing with emotion as she spoke.

Starky pulled the .50 Sharps casing from his pocket
and kissed it. ''Don't fail us, baby,'' he said. ''You're
our ace in the hole.''

''I've got mine, too,'' Gene said, producing the one
he had found in the yard at the ranch. ''Just in case we
need extra proof.''

They all gave their weapons one last check; they had
to be as sure of their defenses as they were of themselves. Of all of them, Janet seemed the most confident
in the role she was about to play. She pulled her
shirttail out and mussed her hair a bit, all the while
looking down at the small cluster of cabins.

They rode down the little flat next to the Yellowstone and into the wood yard. The only sign of life
was a chestnut horse lazily switching flies in front of a
good-sized cabin. This had to be the saloon run by
Crazy Alice that the kid had told them about at the
Powder River. On a stool near the door sat a frail man
who looked to be in his late twenties. He crooked his
neck at an odd angle and looked up at them from a piece
of wood he was whittling. He was no doubt Scully,
Crazy Alice's son. Crazy Alice had to be inside.

They tied their horses and moved into the saloon
under the watchful eye of Scully, who twitched his
neck nervously as they went by him. His face and
clothes looked like neither had ever seen soap and
water. He was unshaven, with a scraggly little beard
dotted through with acne. His eyes bored into their
backs as they went past him.

The inside was cool and dank with the smell of stale
liquor and old food. The back door was open, and light
poured across a dirt-covered wood floor spotted with
liquor spills and old tobacco plugs. A large oil painting

of a nearly naked woman hung slightly to one side above the bar. She was covered with a film of dust, and a long scratch reached across the flimsy scarlet cloth that covered her middle. She lay with her head tilted back at an inviting angle across a plush couch. A few well-placed bullet holes had found their way onto various parts of the picture as well as through a large mirror underneath.

A squat woman with a round, puffy face got up from a deck of cards in one corner and ground her toothless gums as she moved behind the bar. She studied them in silence while she adjusted a filthy, loose-hanging dress that had been inching up while she had been sitting. She had one bad eye that kept wandering back and forth of center to the outside corner of the socket. Her large cheeks pinched up into a scowl as she studied them. It wasn't hard to see why they called her Crazy Alice.

"It's sure been a cool spring, ain't it?" Starky ventured.

She shrugged while she raised an arm rolled with fat and ran her fingers into her tangled mat of gray hair and began to scratch.

"You sell meals here?" Starky asked.

She brought her fingers down out of her hair and studied what she had collected under the nails from her scratching, cocking her head sideways to get a better view from the bad eye. She looked up and said, "This ain't a hash house." The words were garbled as she forced them out of her toothless mouth.

"We'll pay you," said Starky.

"Got some beans in the back I could heat up out here on the stove," she said. "That's all; you can take it or leave it." Her right eye wandered back and forth from looking at them to the corner of its socket.

"Bring them out," said Starky.

"They're two days old," she said, scratching her head again.

Starky shrugged. "They'll do."

She grunted and turned for the back room, the fat on her arms and body pushing against her dress as she moved.

"Starky, I'm really not that hungry," Janet groaned.

Starky grinned. "We're not about to try the food here. I just want some time to look around in this place before I ask if anybody's been through in the last couple of days."

Janet said, "From the looks of things, no one has cleaned up in here for over a year. How can you tell who's been here and when?"

Starky winked. "Some of the tobacco stains will be fresher than the rest."

"I don't like the looks of that scummy bastard outside," Gene put in. "I don't think he's there now, but I don't like him even a little bit."

"Listen," Starky said, putting a finger to his lips. "There's someone in the back with that woman."

They could hear the low sound of voices coming from the back room where Crazy Alice had gone. No doubt Scully had gone around to the back to talk things over with her. They couldn't hear what was being said, but the hissing sound Scully was making while he talked made it clear that he didn't like them at all.

"This is getting on my nerves," Gene said. "I wonder if they got any idea why we're here?"

"I doubt it," Starky answered. "Most likely they just don't enjoy having strangers show up. If you were mixed up with horse thieves, would you?"

"I guess you're right. But it seems to me that they're more than just a little bit uneasy. That Scully might be trying to get us in on more than we planned."

Crazy Alice returned with a large soot-blackened pot and let it drop on the stove near the bar. The sound of walking out front announced Scully's return to the stool near the door.

"That's Scully," said Crazy Alice, poking some wood into the stove. "He's my boy. He gets a little edgy when strangers stop by." She worked at the fire to see that it stayed lit and clanged the lid back in place. "Ain't much here," she said as she moved over behind the bar and grabbed a wooden spoon from a pile of dirty dishes. "I ain't got time to fix you more."

She went back and stuck the dirty wooden spoon into the beans while Scott wondered what the fly population would be like in that place after another few weeks of warm weather.

"A little is better than nothing," Starky told her. "We've come a long ways, and our bellies are empty."

She ambled behind the bar and stopped across from them. Her eye kept twitching, and the fat on her arms shook when she placed her palms on top of the makeshift counter top. Her smell was choking, and Scott wondered how long it had been since she had touched a pan of water.

"Need somethin' to drink while you're waitin'?" she asked.

"Whiskey," Starky said right away. "We've got a thirst that won't die, and whiskey will kill anything there is."

When Crazy Alice had turned around, he gave them a quick wink. It was assurance against worrying about the streaked glasses she was reaching for behind the bar.

Crazy Alice set the bottle on the bar. "You plan on drinkin' it all?" she asked, tilting her head sideways to study them with her good eye.

"Just a few drinks," Starky said.

She rubbed a hand over her puffy face and said, "Let's see, the beans and drinks together comes to four dollars."

"What?" Gene blurted out.

"I need four dollars," she said, slapping her pudgy hands against the bar to emphasize the point.

"We're not about to drink that much," Gene informed her.

She wrapped her chubby fingers around the neck of the bottle. "Four dollars," she insisted, her toothless mouth curling into a scowl.

"That's not too bad," said Starky agreeably. "This is a long way out to bring liquor." He gave Gene a small nod as he reached into his pocket for some coins.

Gene blew out his breath and threw down some loose change while Janet turned away in disgust. Scott reached into his pocket, and soon there was a pile of silver on the top of the bar. Crazy Alice let out a small laugh and licked her lips. She greedily collected the money as if someone was going to beat her to it and stuffed it into a pouch on her leg under the greasy dress.

"We need another glass," said Janet firmly, noticing that there were only three on the bar.

Crazy Alice scratched her tangled hair and reached for another glass with the same hand. Janet reached over quickly for the glass and poured it half full of whiskey. She sloshed it around in the glass a moment and tossed it out across the room, where it made a dull splat on the floor. After lifting the glass to the light and looking through it, she poured it full and took a good-sized swallow. She let it go down without flinching and then took another.

Crazy Alice let out a grunt and stared at Janet for a while. "It's kind of funny, you three out here with a woman," she drawled, her toothless mouth working all the time as if she were chewing a big wad of gum. "You ain't from around these parts, are you?"

Starky took the opportunity to break their plan in. "Looking for horses to buy. Know anybody that's got any for sale?"

She looked hard at Starky, her mouth and bad eye still going. "Horses you want, eh?" she finally said. "Ain't there none where you come from?" She was squinting hard.

"We were told someone over here maybe had some for sale," Starky said, lifting the whiskey to his lips with his eyes on her all the time. "In fact, we heard a man named Taggert was selling them right along."

"Who told you that?" she asked, still squinting and working her gums.

"A friend of ours named Jack Stringer mentioned it," Starky said while he refilled his glass. "People who know him good call him Stringer Jack. He told us we could find some of Taggert's bunch here. You know anything about that?"

She studied all of them a moment and turned back to the stove. In a moment, she had the wooden spoon in her chubby fingers and was working it through the beans with short, choppy strokes. "How about the girl?" she asked without turning. "You got her along for flatbackin' or somethin'?"

Janet was standing next to Scott with her drink in her hand. He could feel the energy come pouring out of her as she tightened up. She set her glass down on the bar, and Scott grabbed her arm to hold her back.

"You got no call to say a thing like that," Janet said hotly. "I'm not as cheap as someone like you."

Crazy Alice turned and gave Janet a toothless sneer while her bad eye worked its way back into her skull.

"Sure, honey," she said with a cackle. "I know; that's what they all say. I'll bet you bed all of them at once." She turned back to the beans.

Scott had to hold Janet back again.

"Now, if you was to take up with me," she went on, "I'd bet you'd get a better shake than with them three runnin' horses all the time. My girls got a nice place down at the end cabin, and—"

Scully jumped up from his place outside the door and stuck his head in. "They're here, Ma," he yelled to Crazy Alice. "I told you this would happen!"

Crazy Alice was furious at being interrupted for something she considered trivial.

"Now they'll think we—" Scully started again.

"Shut up," Crazy Alice ordered as loud as her harsh voice would go. "I told you I'd handle this. Now get back out there!" She settled down a bit and told them, "Like I said, Scully's a bit edgy. Just anybody happens along, and he goes and gets upset."

They heard horses outside, and in a moment two men barged through the doorway. It was Bull Taggert and Rico LaFarge. Bull looked even bigger close up than Scott had noticed under the trees on the Powder River. He was massive; just the sight of him was enough to take a person's breath away. He had a big red beard that moved on his face as he worked at a mouthful of tobacco. He wore a ratty fur cap that looked like it was nearly eaten by lice. The rest of him was a mixture of various kinds of fur also, which made him look like some sort of giant redheaded bear.

Rico LaFarge had a long, thin face that harbored a pair of little black eyes. He kept his lips in a tight line that didn't seem to be long enough for a mouth; it looked like a thin scratch across somebody's upper chin. The rest of him was as bony as his face, and the fingers of his right hand were held in sort of a half curl, as if they were used to the butt of a revolver.

"Hey, Alice, we need some whiskey," Bull shouted, slamming his huge body into the bar and looking Scott and the rest of them over with a scowl.

Crazy Alice walked behind the bar to where the two of them stood. "Good to see you boys again," she said, spreading her mouth into a smile that showed only red gums. "Been missin' you."

Bull looked from her to Scott's group and back again. "We've been busy," he said, sprouting a grin through the whiskers and squeezing one of her flabby breasts. "But we ain't too busy to come by now and again. I smell beans." He raised his nose into the air and sniffed.

"You big stud," Crazy Alice cackled. "You always got to eat before you do anythin'." She gave his beard a girlish tug and went back to the stove.

"You must be Bull Taggert," Starky said. "Can I buy you two boys a drink?"

Bull reached over and took their bottle. He tipped it and poured down a large swallow before he handed it to LaFarge. "Who's askin'?" he demanded in a mean tone with a chilly edge to it.

"Jack Stringer," Starky replied calmly, tipping his whiskey.

Bull spat a stream of tobacco juice across the bar into the liquor bottles lined along the shelf. "I don't see him here." He grabbed the bottle from LaFarge and tilted it up again.

"He don't need to be here," Starky said confidently. "He sent us to do some business with you."

"He didn't send you to do no business with us," Bull growled.

Starky met his stare. "Well, I guess if you boys

don't deal in horses, then maybe we got the wrong place. We might as well ride on out." He looked to the others, and they all started to move away from the bar.

"Hold on, now," Bull ordered, moving his massive frame in front of them. "Why should I think you know Stringer?"

"Because I told you we do," Starky said bluntly. "Now, do we deal or not? We ain't got all day here."

Bull moved back over to the bar. Scott had been watching LaFarge while Bull and Starky had been talking. The fight at the Powder River came back to him as he read the cold expression in the gunman's eyes. He could hear the kid yelling for LaFarge to stop and help him with his wounded brother, and he could hear LaFarge's grainy voice telling the kid to leave his brother for dead. The man looked like he wanted to kill again, as soon as he could. His little black eyes showed it; they were hard and unseeing, and he kept them squinted and darting around like a caged rat.

LaFarge had been watching Gene at the same time, measuring him and wondering how easy it would be to kill him—or if it would be easy. Gene knew what LaFarge's thoughts were and returned a cold stare of his own. It made LaFarge nervous.

Crazy Alice left the pot of beans a minute and came over across the bar from LaFarge. Her mouth was working, and when her good eye split off to look at LaFarge, the bad one slipped over on Scott, making his stomach jump.

"Carla's been askin' when you'd be back around again, Rico," she said, her toothless mouth holding an awkward grin. She put her hand inside her dress and scratched under her arm. "Maybe you'd like to go down to the cabin."

LaFarge let out a stupid laugh that came out all at

once. For the first time, the inside of his mouth was visible; it was lined with sharp yellow teeth.

Bull jabbed him with a big elbow. "Stick around."

"It'll just take a minute," LaFarge argued.

"I said stick around!"

The yellow teeth went back under the small, tight lips, and LaFarge shifted his eyes from Bull to the group of them, as if to say he didn't want anything of what they had just seen or heard to get out.

"So you're part of Stringer's bunch, eh?" Bull said, reaching into his shirt pocket and pulling out an empty rifle cartridge. "Have you ever seen one of these?" He set the cartridge down on the bar in front of Starky and gave him a challenging glare.

Starky reached into his pocket and brought out an empty cartridge of his own. "Stringer sent it along with me," he said, placing it on the bar next to the one Bull had set there. "He said your pappy gave it to him as sort of a callin' card."

Bull studied Starky and picked up the cartridges. He put the rims together and compared the .50-caliber imprints and the paint.

Satisfied, he tossed Starky's cartridge back on the bar and returned his own to his pocket.

"What are you doin' down in this country so early?" he asked through a burp. "The old man wasn't expectin' you for a couple days yet."

Starky played it cool. "There's been a change of plans. Stringer sent us down early."

Bull took another gulp of whiskey and burped again. "He did? So why didn't he come like he told the old man he would?"

"He's in some trouble," Starky explained. "He figures it's best if he lays low for a while. You see—"

"You're lyin'," came a loud voice from the doorway. "That ain't true!" It was Scully, standing in the shadows just inside the door.

"What the hell you say?" Bull demanded.

The inside of Scott's stomach turned into a knot, and he could hear Janet suck her breath in quickly beside him. It looked like Gene's fear of Scully making trouble for them was about to become a reality.

Chapter 11

Scully came out of the shadows and snuck around to where Crazy Alice was stirring beans. "Ma, they ain't none of Stringer's bunch," he said in a high-pitched whine. "We never saw them with Stringer yesterday when he brought them horses through."

"What horses?" Bull asked.

"Stringer came through with some horses from a raid up by Fort Buford," Scully explained. "He stopped here to see Ma's girls and said he would send some boys back down in two, maybe three days when he got back up to the Missouri."

"Things have changed," Starky told him. "There's lots of trouble brewing around here. We've got to move those horses fast."

Scully was shaking his head. "Hell, you weren't even with them when they came through yesterday."

"We met them at the line cabin on the Musselshell last night," Starky said. He looked to Bull. "You know, the place he sometimes trades at?"

Scully kept shaking his head. "He never said nothin' about goin' over there. He said he was goin' straight north from here."

LaFarge's eyes darted around the room in quick,

searching glances that always stopped at Bull for his reaction. Bull was silent, but his face wore an ugly frown.

Starky picked up the bottle from in front of Bull. His hand was steady as a rock as he poured his glass full. He slowly drained it, and his voice took on a twinge of meanness to let everybody know where he stood. "I don't see why we have to put up with some half-baked runt when we come here on a job." He turned, and his eyes pierced into Scully, making him take a few steps back toward Crazy Alice. She kept stirring the beans but took on the look of a she-bear protecting a cub.

"And I can't figure why this damned place ain't a bit more hospitable," he went on, his tone edging into a growl. "All we've heard since we got to this rathole is a bunch of *crap*!" He slammed the bottle down heavily on the bar, and the sound rang out loud and sharp.

Everyone jumped, even Bull. The huge man's eyes popped wide open with surprise, and he studied Starky a moment as if to figure out what he was made of. Gene wore a small grin on his face and moved away from the bar to keep everybody spread apart in case any trouble started. LaFarge watched him and shuffled from one foot to the other nervously, flexing his fingers as if keeping them ready for use at any time. Scott felt a firm feeling of confidence well up; now the upper hand was theirs, and both Bull and LaFarge knew it.

"Now," Starky started in again, his voice more moderate but still firm, "we usually work the Judith Basin country. Due to some problems down there, we just moved up with Stringer's main bunch."

Bull grunted and picked up the whiskey bottle again. After a long swallow, he came out of the shock of Starky's outbreak. "What's this trouble you've been talkin' about here?"

"Ever hear of Bill Cantrell?" Starky asked.

Bull nodded. "They call him Floppin' Bill. He used to be a wood hawk up on the Missouri."

"That's the one," said Starky. "Now he's getting paid wages to look out for other people's horses. From what I hear, he's taking it pretty serious. And there's another one they call the White Bandit. He means business. Things are hot around here now."

"Ain't none of that true, I tell you," Scully squeaked. "They ain't even with Stringer."

Gene turned toward Scully, and his face was deeply flushed. "Now, I think we've heard just about enough from this son of a bitch here!" His teeth were gritted as he spoke, and Scully got a look of fear on his face. "I want you to get over to that table and sit down." Gene had his arm pointed rigidly toward the table Crazy Alice had been sitting at when they had come in. "Move!"

Scully looked to Crazy Alice for help.

"You'd best go on over, son," she advised him.

"But, Ma—"

"I said move," Gene blared.

All the while LaFarge was waiting for Bull to make a move so that he could start shooting. At the same time, he could feel Gene's and Starky's eyes watching his every move. Bull knew the best thing would be to wait and see how things turned out between Scully and Gene.

Scully huffed past Gene to the table. He stood in front of a chair and pointed his arm as he spoke. "You just wait; Stringer told me none of them knew how to get into Makoshika. He said he needed a map. You never said nothin' to us about no—"

"I said shut up!" Gene barked. "I swear to God, one more peep out of you, and I'll blow your head off, horse deal or not!"

Scully was still boiling mad, but he sat down without

another word. He looked over to Bull and LaFarge for support and didn't get any. They were both watching Gene go back to the bar.

"It riles me when people can't keep quiet while other folks talk," he explained as he picked up his drink and shook his head. "I hear one more word, and he's a dead son of a bitch."

Crazy Alice lumbered behind the bar to where Bull was handing the bottle to LaFarge. "You should've said somethin', Bull," she garbled in a low irritated tone. "He had no call to talk to Scully like that."

"Weren't none of my affair," Bull said with a shrug. "They showed me Pa's rifle shell. Only us and Stringer's bunch has got them. Scully had no call to spout off like that."

Crazy Alice looked over at Gene and turned her toothless mouth up into a frown so that the fat on her face pushed around her eyes. "Maybe so," she hissed. "But Scully ain't usually wrong about things. Folks think he's stupid 'cause he don't say much, but when he does, it ain't just to hear himself talk."

"Fetch them beans over here," Bull ordered. "Just bring the pot over and set it down." He hooked the wad of tobacco he had been chewing out of his mouth with a big forefinger and flung it onto the board floor behind him.

Crazy Alice went past Gene and grabbed the steaming pot as if she wanted to crush it. She sat it down in front of Bull with a loud thump and started for the back room with her toothless face twisted.

"Hold on," Bull yelled after her. "There ain't enough beans here to feed no goddamn mouse. Get another pot and put them on."

"I'll see if I can find some," she said in a low tone as she pounded into the back room. It didn't sound like she was eager to get any more for him.

Bull grabbed the big wooden spoon and ladled a pile of beans into his mouth. He leaned over, spat them back into the pot with a big blow of air, and yelled, "Hot!" Some of the beans had caught in his beard on the way down, and he was flicking them off onto the top of the bar with his fingers. He wiped his hands on his pants and grabbed the whiskey bottle.

All the while LaFarge was studying them with a suspicious look on his face. It was plain he had believed Scully, but he just hadn't figured out how they had come across a .50 Sharps rifle shell with red paint on it.

Bull set the bottle down and turned to Starky. "What's this about trouble brewin' with the cowpunchers, now?"

Starky downed his drink and said, "You boys don't get around much, do you? Word has it that old Granville Stuart down in the Judiths is gettin' the stockmen organized against stock thieves. And from what I gather, they ain't bothering to include no lawmen in their group, just those with a stomach for hangings."

"That true?" Bull asked without emotion. He didn't seem surprised. No doubt he was remembering what had happened to them at the Powder River.

"You're damn right," Starky said with force. "They mean business. From what we heard, they've been planning some kind of raid. It don't sound good."

Bull blew on a spoonful of beans to cool them off and nibbled at a few on the end. "Do they know who they're after?"

"That's what we've been trying to tell you," Starky said. "They've got a list put together, and Stringer's right near the top of it. I heard the Taggert name brought up, too. I don't know how many men they've got, but I do know Stringer is worried enough to get the hell out of the country for a while.''

Bull and LaFarge were silent. Bull walked away from the bar slowly with his head bowed in thought. He gave one of the tables a shattering kick that sent it crashing into the table where Scully was sitting. Scully jerked a little and cowered down into the chair while Bull's loud voice boomed a line of profanity.

''What the hell's the matter with you?'' LaFarge asked.

''We got so damn many horses, they're crawlin' up one another's back down there, and more comin' in,'' Bull growled. ''Now we find out there's stranglers and regulators strung out all over the country, and you ask me what the matter is.'' He turned from LaFarge and slammed a big boot into another chair. ''Pa ain't about to like this, not one little bit.''

''Ain't you got any way of getting rid of those horses?'' Starky asked.

''Not right away,'' Bull answered. ''We just picked up some of that stock the last couple of days, and hell, the brands ain't even been changed on none of them yet.''

Starky challenged him. ''What? Stringer was planning on getting horses with worked-over brands.''

''I know it.'' Bull hesitated before he explained. ''Our man that changes brands, well, he left us a few days back. I guess he got edgy or somethin'.''

Bull wasn't kidding anybody. Scott knew he must have been one of the outlaws they had killed at the Powder River fight.

''None of them got their brands changed yet?'' Starky asked.

Bull shook his head. ''You know anythin' about brands?''

Starky laughed. ''Hell, no. But I got a friend over on the Musselshell who does. Maybe we can still make that deal with your bunch.''

Bull relaxed a moment and thought about it. ''You say you're interested in maybe takin' those horses off our hands?''

''Maybe,'' said Starky.

''You payin' the same money as before?''

''Well, we couldn't pay as much, since it's going to cost us money to get the brands worked over.''

Bull stiffened. He didn't like the idea of losing out on any money. ''They're good horses,'' he said.

LaFarge spoke up. ''Now, Bull, you can't go makin' no deals without your old man's say-so. He'd get plumb up—''

''I know it!'' Bull exploded. ''I ain't about to do no tradin' now. What the hell's the matter with you?'' He was standing over LaFarge now, with his huge bulk pressing him into the bar. ''You'll get paid no matter what we do with the horses. You goddamn gunslicks don't give a holler in hell for nothin' but your wages, do you?'' Bull was crowding LaFarge harder all the time, and the color of his cheeks was the same shade as his big crop of beard. ''I should just squash your guts out right now.''

''No, Bull,'' LaFarge pleaded. ''I just—''

''You just do what you're told from now on,'' Bull commanded, glowering down into LaFarge's shrunken face. ''It seems like you're always spoutin' off out of turn. You just do what you're hired for and leave all the talkin' to me. Got that?''

''Sure, Bull,'' LaFarge managed. ''I didn't mean—''

''Just remember what I said,'' Bull broke in. ''I'm sick of you forgettin' who the hell the boss is around here.''

''You're the boss, Bull,'' LaFarge said. ''You're the boss.''

Bull eased off and grabbed the bottle from the bar. He tipped it straight up, rolling his eyes shut while he drank. He set it down, and the sting made his eyes seem wetter and meaner as he blew his breath out loudly and shuddered as the whiskey went down. LaFarge looked little and beaten. He kept his eyes on the top of the bar and wouldn't look anywhere else. It was easy to tell that he wanted a drink but was afraid to ask Bull for the bottle.

Bull started in on his kettle of beans. He spooned a mouthful through his beard and turned to Starky. "Let's talk some more about those horses," he said, slobbering beans out of his mouth and onto his beard as he spoke.

"We'd like to pick them up as soon as we can," Starky said. "There ain't a lot of time to get them out of the country."

Bull swallowed his mouthful of beans and ladled another in. "We still ain't got this money thing settled. The deal was twenty dollars a head."

"You get fifteen," Starky told him. "I told you it costs money to get brands changed."

Bull took a few moments to scrape the last of the beans from the bottom of the kettle. He slurped the last bits of bean and juice off the wooden spoon, and it made a sticky sucking sound in his mouth as he talked to Starky. "Some of them got changed brands, some of them don't. We'll give you all of them, brands changed or not, for eighteen dollars a head."

Starky nodded. "If it's good horseflesh, we'll pay it."

"You're damn right you'll pay it," Bull said, still chewing. "All our horses are good."

"How many you got?" Starky asked.

"About fifty or sixty head. You got money enough?"

Starky filled his whiskey again. "We've got plenty of money."

Bull pushed the empty bean pot back and cleaned his mouth and beard with a quick wipe of his sleeve. "I'd kind of like to see your money."

Starky took a deep breath and turned sideways to the bar so that he was facing Bull. In a firm tone he said, "I don't show nobody any money for a damn thing until I see what I'm paying for. If the son of a bitch I'm dealing with at the time don't like it that way, then I don't deal."

Bull drew his eyes into a squint. "Ain't you a bit up in years to be talkin' so rough?"

Starky gave him a confident little grin. "Years don't mean a damn thing. The smart ones learn that when they're young. That way they live to get older; simple as that."

Bull turned around to LaFarge. "He sounds pretty tough, don't he?"

LaFarge was licking his lips nervously with his eyes on Gene and Scott. "Seems to me like it would be easy for him to talk that way, since he's got lots of younger friends to back him up."

Starky moved away from the bar and looked around Bull at LaFarge. "From what I've seen of you today, you should stick to doing the laundry and leave the talking to the menfolk."

LaFarge's face flushed, and his eyes turned coal black. His small mouth tightened until it almost vanished as the muscles in his jaw popped out full from his face.

"Maybe you've got some laundry to do now," Gene put in.

LaFarge turned his eyes on Gene. Before, LaFarge couldn't have proven anything to anybody in the room by gunning Starky down; it would only make him look small to shoot an older man. But now Gene was involved, and that was another matter.

"You're talkin' out of turn," LaFarge warned. "Or maybe you were just lookin' for trouble."

"Now, hold on," Bull broke in, putting a brawny arm in front of LaFarge. "We can't go shootin' people we're doin' business with. Maybe we should just teach them a lesson so they know who they're dealin' with." He was looking at Starky with his mouth drawn into a smirk.

"I think you need the lesson, fat boy," Starky said with a mean edge. "You're just too big for your britches."

Bull's eyes widened with surprise.

Gene moved over to Starky. "You don't plan on fighting him, I hope?"

Starky brushed him off. "Gene, stay out of this. I called the play."

Bull had an evil grin on his face. "You ain't serious?"

"Tell you what I'll do," said Starky. "I'll even give you the first punch, since you won't be remembering the last one."

Bull's face clouded with anger. Starky didn't budge an inch; he was determined to prove what he had said. Crazy Alice ambled out from the back of the room with an evil sneer etched into the fat on her face. She most likely had seen what Bull could do to a man some time before, maybe more than once. Scott and Janet moved away from the bar to give them room, and Gene stood watching LaFarge to make sure it was a fair fight. With the anger that was evident in each man's face, it was plain that there definitely was going to be a fight. Somehow, Scott felt this would make or break their effort to get the horses back. All there was to do now was to see who came out the winner.

Chapter 12

Starky looked calm and deliberate, waiting for Bull to make the first move. Bull swaggered away from the bar and adjusted his clothes as if he was going to make a speech, shaking his head at the same time; he evidently couldn't believe that someone could be so crazy. He even laughed. He quit laughing when Starky told him he'd better get his one punch in while he still had the chance.

Then Scully started yelling, "Come on, Bull. Kill him! Let's go, Bull!" He let out a high-pitched cackle.

Bull lunged at Starky, with determination etched on his face. With surprising swiftness, Starky moved aside and sent a fast right hand into Bull's huge middle. It was a quick, darting stroke that sank in deep and knocked Bull completely off balance.

For a moment, Bull was helpless. He was too big to hurt very much with just one blow, but Starky's solid punch to his middle had taken him by surprise and stunned him. He stood with his huge frame half doubled over and was frozen there with the wind partially knocked out of him. For Starky, that moment meant his last easy chance to do further damage to the giant. He knew that if Bull ever got hold of him, there would be no getting away.

Starky used that one moment so well that the rest of the room stood in shocked silence. He moved so quickly in that split second that it seemed he must be much younger than he looked; and for Bull Taggert, it brought on more pain than he had probably ever had to endure in his entire life.

He gave Bull a solid kick to the back of the knee that knocked the big man off balance. As Bull slumped sideways, his chin popped up, and Starky sent a powerful blow with his forearm straight up into his throat. Bull's eyes walled out and up into his head as he clutched his throat and tried to yell. Gagging, he crashed into the tables and lay groaning on his side, finished in a matter of seconds by a man half his size and over twice his age.

LaFarge and Scully looked around as if they didn't know what was happening. Crazy Alice lost the sneer on her face, and the fat dropped instead into an expression of complete surprise.

Gene went over to Starky and clapped him on the back. "Where did you learn to fight like that?" he asked, the respect evident in his voice. "He didn't even touch you."

Starky looked disgustedly down at Bull. "I don't take any pleasure in it, but sometimes it has to be done."

It took quite a while for Bull to get up and around again. His voice came back hoarse at first and gradually worked itself out to normal. LaFarge was trying to help him but wasn't having much luck; Bull was indignant about the whole thing and wanted to be left alone. No one had ever done anything like that to him in his life, and it was hard for him to get over the shock.

It was only the beginning of what they had come for, and Scott knew that the rest was going to be a life-or-death struggle. Bull and LaFarge hadn't been put in their place by what had just happened; it had only served to ignite them. The look in their eyes said they would settle things only by killing—that was their life-style. But both men knew they would have to play their cards right and wait until they had gotten what they wanted first. When the time came, Bull would want another chance at Starky, most likely from the back. In the meantime, Starky was facing him, and Bull kept a respectful distance.

"You ready to talk horses now?" Starky asked.

"I need some more whiskey," Bull said.

Crazy Alice found another bottle and set it on the bar next to Bull. She watched him jerk the cork out with her mouth working. Then she said, "Now what do you think about takin' their side against Scully?"

Bull put the bottle down, and his face went red again. "I don't want to hear no more about that, understand?" he bellowed. He picked up the empty bean pot and gave it a tremendous throw against the wood stove in the corner. It made a dull clang and splattered half-dried bean juice all over the stove and floor. Bull raged on. "Goddamnit, I thought I told you to fix me up some more beans!"

She shrunk back and nodded. Her bad eye seemed to go wild in her head.

"Now get the hell back in there and do as you're told!" Bull ordered.

Crazy Alice turned and started for the back room, clutching nervously at her filthy dress. She stooped and retrieved the bean pan with a heavy grunt and surveyed the damage before moving into the back room.

"So how soon can you take those horses off our hands, if we was to deal?" Bull asked.

"Just as soon as we can get down there to get them," Starky answered.

"Let's talk a little more about it," said Bull, as if he

wasn't sure of things yet or even knew whether he was still interested in selling them.

"To hell with it," Starky said disgustedly. He walked from the bar and started toward the door, motioning for the rest of them to follow. "This is the damndest thing I ever saw."

"Wait," said Bull. "Why the hell are you leavin'?"

"You ain't even got final say on whether or not we deal, and you're standing there asking us a lot of stupid questions," Starky told him. "I think we're all wasting our time."

"Now, hold on," Bull pleaded. "I just want to know if we'll get paid, that's all."

Starky shook his head as if he couldn't believe what he had just heard. "Well, I'll be damned. Your bunch is supposed to have thirty head of horses with their brands changed, ready for us to pick up, and you two show up with your hands in your pockets like you just got kicked out of school with the word that you don't have them ready. Now *you're* asking us if *we'll* make good on a deal. That don't make much sense to me."

Bull was silent.

"Maybe you'd better explain that a little better to us," Starky went on. "I'm not so damned sure you've got horses down there to deal."

"Oh, we've got them to deal," Bull said quickly. "I already said we could give you close to sixty head. We just ain't got the brands changed yet."

"That's why I think we're wasting our time," Starky explained. "We might be a little early, but you can't change the brands on sixty horses in less than a week's time. If I can't get that friend of mine on the Musselshell to go along with helpin' us out, Stringer's going to be damn mad—and all because of you."

Bull slammed his massive hand down on the bar and cursed. "Look, we ran into some trouble on Powder

River a few days back. Maybe it was that White Bandit, I don't know. But we lost a bunch of horses and some of our men. We're runnin' damned shorthanded now."

Crazy Alice came over to where Bull was and broke in. "I think Scully has something you might want to hear," she said, giving Starky a suspicious look.

Scott and Gene both looked over to the table where Scully had been sitting. He was gone. He must have taken the opportunity to sneak out during the confusion after the fight. No doubt Scully had been talking to Crazy Alice in the back about the map he had drawn to lead Jack Stringer's bunch into Makoshika, and now it looked like he was determined to make Bull and LaFarge listen to him. The only thing that was against him was Bull's desire to talk horses.

"We're busy here," Bull told Crazy Alice with disgust. "You get back over to them beans, and I'll tell you when I want to hear from you or Scully. Got that?"

Crazy Alice frowned and turned back to the stove. She mumbled something under her breath about Bull wishing he would have listened and began pounding the wooden spoon through the fresh batch of heating beans as if she was trying to churn the life out of them.

A sound at the doorway drew everyone's attention. A thin wisp of a girl with scraggly brown hair walked into the room. Her hair kept falling down across her eyes, and she was constantly trying to control it by tossing her head and brushing it back with her hands.

LaFarge's face broke into the same ugly grin he had worn when Crazy Alice came over to him just after they had arrived. "Carla," he said, "I was meanin' to come see you."

She returned his smile and moved over to his side. He put an arm around her, and she gave him a quick kiss on the cheek.

"What are you doin' up here, Carla?" Crazy Alice asked. "You're supposed to be gettin' your rest."

"Oh, I just had to see who owned that beautiful yellow horse outside," she said. "He's got your saddle on him, Rico. Is he yours?"

"Just got him," LaFarge answered. "Ain't he somethin'?"

Janet's mouth dropped open. She moved over by LaFarge and the girl and said, "I love horses. Can I go look at him?"

"He ain't for sale," said LaFarge.

"I just want to look." Janet went out, and in a moment she was back again.

Scott watched her expression. There was no doubt it was her horse, Clipper; he could tell it in her expression, though she hid her feelings from everyone else. Gene and Starky had a pretty good idea why she had taken so much interest, but they still couldn't be sure by the way she acted when she came back. Her gladness at finding the horse alive and well and the anger and frustration of seeing someone else's saddle on its back was hidden well. Scott barely detected that little glint in her eye that she got when she was determined to get something done.

"He sure is a pretty one," she said. "Sure you don't want to sell him?"

LaFarge shook his head.

Janet let it go at that. She was too smart to ask him where he had gotten it or to carry on any further conversation. As it was, LaFarge wasn't suspicious at her interest in the horse.

"All my girls like horses, too," Crazy Alice commented from where she stood at the stove. "I think you'd fit right in with us here. Can't see why you'd want to be runnin' all over the country like you are now. You'll just get yourself shot up one of these days.''

Janet walked over by her, keeping a straight face. ''I've been thinking about that. Are you serious about wanting me to go to work here?''

Crazy Alice beamed. ''Why, sure I am.''

''What do I have to do to go to work for you?'' Janet asked.

''Well, just come on with me to the back room, and let's see what you've got.''

Janet said, ''I can show you what I've got right here.''

In one motion, she pulled back and slammed her fist heavily into Crazy Alice's jaw. Crazy Alice let out a wail of pain and tumbled backward to the floor.

''I don't want to hear any more from you about that,'' Janet said, standing over her. ''You understand?''

Crazy Alice looked up from the floor and nodded her head feebly.

''A real fightin' bunch, ain't you?'' Bull observed from his place at the bar.

Just then the doorway filled again. This time it was Scully, and he was back with a piece of paper folded in his hand. ''I've got somethin' here to show you,'' he said to Bull. ''This is that map I told you Stringer's boys wanted.''

''Yeah, sure,'' Bull said. He turned his attention to the stove. ''Bring the rest of them beans over.''

Scott and Gene both tightened. Scully was going to make trouble if he convinced Bull about his story. Right then LaFarge was busy with the girl at the corner of the bar and wasn't paying a lot of attention to what was going on. It was time to make a move.

While Crazy Alice was working to get back on her feet, Janet quickly picked up the new pot of steaming beans from the stove and started over to Bull with them. They bubbled and popped in the big pot as she carried them. Scully was just opening the paper he had brought in when Janet threw the beans flush into Bull's face.

The big man had taken them with his eyes open, and he roared in pain. He stumbled back from the bar, clutching his face and eyes and trying to scrape the steaming beans out of his beard. Janet quickly slammed the heavy pot over LaFarge's head, and he staggered backward into the wall, dazed by the blow. Crazy Alice rushed over with a coarse stream of ugly words, and Janet turned the pot on her, leaving her senseless on the floor with her toothless mouth gaping.

Gene had his gun out and was firing rounds into Scully while he screamed in a high-pitched tone that curdled the blood. Scully jerked with the bullets and piled heavily into the tables back from the bar. Scott had his own gun out, waiting for Bull to come at them, but Bull's face was too badly burned, and he could only roll on the floor in pain.

The saloon girl, Carla, was beside LaFarge, trying to help him. He took the opportunity to grab her and hold her in front of himself as a shield.

"I don't want to see anybody follow me out this door," he said, holding his gun to her ear. "I see anybody and she's dead."

Gene raised his gun.

"Don't do it," Janet yelled. "He'll kill her. He means it!"

"I've got a job to do," Gene argued.

"For God's sake," Janet pleaded. "Put that gun down."

LaFarge was breathing in short, heavy breaths with his small mouth squeezed tight. His eyes were dark and unseeing, as if he were acting on instincts from within. When Gene lowered his gun, he let out a nervous grunt and backed out the door with the saloon girl in front of him. In a moment, a horse was running outside.

"You just ruined our chances at those horses," Gene told Janet hotly.

"He won't get far," Janet said with confidence, and hurried out the door. Gene looked at Scott and Starky with a shrug, and they all followed behind her.

LaFarge was riding as fast as he could by himself. He had carried the saloon girl with him but had dropped her in the trail once he felt safe. What he hadn't counted on was how well the horse had been trained to obey its master.

Janet cupped her hands around her mouth and yelled, "Clipper, hold left!"

The big palomino made a quick right-angle turn that threw LaFarge into a pile on the ground.

"Home, Clipper, home," Janet yelled.

The big palomino came rushing back to Janet, who welcomed him with tears and hugs. Scott and Gene rushed up to where LaFarge was struggling to his feet. Gene cocked his .44 and leveled it.

LaFarge had lost his pistol in the fall. "You wouldn't shoot a man without a gun," he said, a nervous smile on his lips. His hat was gone, and the stringy black hair on his head was in a mess.

"You'd do it," Gene came back.

LaFarge shook his head back and forth. "No, don't."

"Throw him yours," Gene said to Scott.

Scott tossed his pistol at LaFarge's feet. LaFarge kept looking down at it and back up at Gene, breathing quickly again, his eyes wide as if he was about to make a jump off a high building.

"There it is," said Gene. "Or would you rather hang?"

LaFarge's eyes got a wild look to them, and he made

a quick stab for the gun, springing to one side as he came up. As he stood crouched, Gene's .44 exploded. LaFarge dropped the gun and stumbled forward with a gasp. His legs buckled, and he sank down to his knees. His mouth was wide open as if he was trying to scream, but nothing would come out. Gene's second shot slammed into his forehead, and he flopped onto his face like a rag doll.

Back up the street, the saloon girl was sobbing wretchedly while Janet tried to console her and Starky stood close by. Bull had made his way out the door and onto his horse; he was trying to make a getaway out of the bottom into the hills along the river.

"He'll be a sitting duck goin' up that hill," said Gene as he ran for his Winchester.

Bull struggled to stay in his saddle as the horse labored to climb the hill. He was shaking his huge head of red hair, the pain in his eyes from the hot beans driving him crazy.

Gene's first shot tore into the big man's back just below the right shoulder. Bull's head jerked back, but he continued to hold on. Gene levered another round into the barrel, shaking his head and saying to Scott, "I should have a buffalo gun."

The next shot entered Bull's neck just below the base of the skull. The giant instantly stiffened and flopped backwards off the horse, and rolled down the hill. Starky was standing over him when Gene and Scott got there. His huge hands quivered for a moment, and then the giant lay still.

"He's done," said Gene. This giant's eyes had swollen shut, and his entire face was a blotchy red from the hot beans. "Janet did more than her part with those beans."

Starky checked the saddlebags on Bull's horse and found a big wad of bills. "Looks like we've got some money to deal for horses. Now all we need is that map Scully had.''

Inside the saloon, Crazy Alice was a pitiful sight. She had recovered from the blow Janet had dealt her with the bean pot and was wailing over her dead son, rocking him in her arms. His blood had drenched her filthy dress. Starky reached down and pulled the paper map Scully had wanted to show Bull out of his lifeless grasp. Crazy Alice looked up at him without seeing. Both of her eyes were rolling wildly in their sockets. Her mind was completely gone.

''The stakes are high when you go to stealing stock,'' Gene said.

Looking at Crazy Alice and remembering LaFarge and Bull out in the street, Scott said, ''I think I'd rather hang.''

They went back out in front of the saloon and saw the other girls who worked for Crazy Alice standing at a distance, looking on in fear. The girl named Carla was walking slowly toward them.

Janet joined the other three and said, ''She's in a real bad way. She thought that no-good gunman loved her.''

''Yeah, it's too bad,'' Gene agreed, watching her join the others up the street.

''You didn't seem to have any feelings about her earlier,'' Janet said.

''She wouldn't have cared if we all died,'' Gene said coldly. ''Like you said, she thought LaFarge was her man. She's seen him kill before; she was on his side, not ours.''

Janet was silent a moment. She looked into Gene's eyes and said, ''How can you stand this sort of thing? It's awful.''

Gene didn't answer.

Janet's eyes got misty. ''Is what you told me back at

Glendive Creek true? Do you really feel that way about me?''

Gene looked at her and nodded. ''Yes, I meant it, Janet.''

She lowered her head and took a deep breath. ''Gene, I can just see me in her place. I don't want you dying like that.''

Gene took her in his arms. ''Janet, don't think that way.''

''We'll be waiting for you at the horses,'' Scott said as he and Starky left them alone.

As Scott and Starky stood near the horses in front of the saloon, Scott looked up the street to where Gene and Janet stood talking. He said, ''I hope Gene can talk her into turning back now. I'd go with her in a minute. She's got her own horse back, and we can always get more for the ranch.''

Gene and Janet came over and got their horses ready to leave. While Janet changed saddles on her palomino, Gene talked to Scott and Starky.

''Janet's bound and determined to go into that hell-hole Makoshika with us,'' he said. ''She said it's just as dangerous riding back alone as it is being with us. I can't change her mind.''

''I think she's more worried about you than she is about either herself or her horse now,'' Starky said.

They left Crazy Alice rocking her dead son in the saloon and Bull lying in the sagebrush delirious with pain. LaFarge lay cold and still as they rode by him. Stringer's bunch would find them and learn the story from the girls still standing in front of their cabin, but that would be two days away. By then they should have made the deal with Old Man Taggert for the horses and would be well on their way home. They all knew that would be the hardest part of their mission.

Chapter 13

Scully's map was a godsend. The way into Old Man Taggert's horse ranch in Makoshika was more complicated than any of them had ever imagined. The "back door," as the map called it, was a mass of twists and turns that went into the heart of the badlands. Without knowing the way or having it drawn out for him, no one could have found the way in except by accident, and there weren't too many people who were about to ride into country like that unless they had a good reason.

The first leg of the trip took them up Box Elder Creek about three miles, to where Scully had marked a turnoff at the bottom of a small draw. The landmark was a gigantic dead cottonwood with an eagle's nest in the top. They passed under the tree and found the area strewn with small animal bones and feathers from other birds that had been a meal for the young eagles. Their mother flapped out of the nest with a heavy beat of her big, broad wings and let out a sharp cry as she left.

Once out of the bottom, they traversed a large flat Scully had labeled Belle Prairie. It was a broad sandy flat cut through in places by gravelly ridges and draws. Scott saw a lot of the same grass he remembered from the Flint Hills. Big colonies of sandreed and turkeyfoot were mixed in with the shorter-growing needlegrass that had a long curly tail on the seed. It was funny that he should come upon something that reminded him of home at a time like this.

Belle Prairie dropped off into the kind of country that they had first seen while coming across the dead horses a few days earlier. It was an expanse of bare knobs and steep shale slopes that had been cut deep by the rains of a million years. There was still a good amount of grassy flats and timbered slopes that had somehow taken root, but the country was getting rougher by the mile.

The last landmark before they got into the heart of the country was Glendive Creek. Scott remembered the lower end of it where it met the Yellowstone as a peaceful little brook in a pretty green setting of cottonwoods and wild plums. This section was the boundary line between them and the hardest ride Scott would ever make, through country that looked as though it had never been nice to a living creature.

It all seemed the same, as the kid at Powder River had told them it would be. The trail took them up and down and around an uneven and roughly cut pattern of steep hills and washouts. The sides of the nearly vertical coulees were sectioned into layers of dark gray shale with mixed sections of sandstone in the form of open-faced knobs and various rock formations. This gave way to a thin black seam of coal near the very top of the formation. The sides of the hills were a mass of scars from erosion and eons of facing a strong wind. The area looked like nature had gotten mad at one time or another and had heaved an ordinarily gentle landscape up into a mass of broken rocks and tumbled land forms left raw and open to the baking heat of the summers and the bitter cold of the northern winters, and then had taken pity and smoothed over the surface by covering some of the scars with scattered plots of grass and scrag timber wherever it would catch.

The day had passed into evening, and the sun had moved low enough to leave the bottoms of the gullies in shadows. They looked massive and deep as the trail skirted dropoffs and long, steep slopes with nothing but crusted knobs of clay and patches of broken rock to greet them if their horses slipped. They were in a land abandoned by all but Old Man Taggert and his family of thieves.

The time of the year made the rugged badlands as pretty as they would ever be with the brilliance of the spring flowers that poked themselves up in the most unusual places. They grew through cracks in the hardpan clay and arranged themselves in little bouquets among the rocks and weathered cliffs, wherever there was a spot of earth to grow in. Once during a stop to stretch their legs, they picked up rocks with the imprints of strange fish in them along with tiny bone fragments of creatures that had lived there in great numbers at one time, crusted remnants of an age long forgotten.

The badlands had a rugged beauty all their own, but it gave Scott the feeling that hell was swallowing him up.

They had been moving close to two hours since crossing Glendive Creek, when they came to the head of a coulee that was rounded out in dish fashion and was covered with a good stand of green grass that the horses immediately took a liking to. The spot marked the end of the trail on their map and was labeled simply the Bowl. Underneath the title was a short narrative explaining that this was where Old Man Taggert would meet them to lead them into his horse ranch. No doubt

Scully hadn't known the exact way in from here. There
was a good chance that nobody but Taggert's family
knew it.

A little spring ran out of the hillside near the bottom
of the bowl-shaped meadow. They left the horses hobbled to drink and graze while they set up camp. The
evening was peaceful, and the little spring was filled
with small frogs of the species that showed up in every
little puddle and sang their hearts out as soon as the air
got warm enough at night. Mourning doves cooed into
the evening while a family of killdeers scolded loudly
at the invasion of their waterhole, making sharp noises
and running along the edge of the spring on their
spindly little legs. It was a pretty evening that was
broken by a gruff voice that came down from the
hillside above them.

They all looked up to see three riders with their rifles
ready.

"No fancy moves!" one of the men called down.
"Just all stand up slow with your hands in the air."

In a moment, the rider who had spoken rode down
the hill while the other two kept him covered. He
reined in a short distance from them, brought his rifle
up, and rested the butt on his leg. His clothes were
ragged and worn, and he looked down at them from
under a floppy brimmed hat with eyes that showed
meanness clear through. A leering smile worked itself
across his unshaven face as he watched Janet for a long
moment. In a display of self-consciousness, the smile
vanished, and he ran a finger along the top of his nose,
which had an ugly scar that traced almost the entire
length of the nostril along the left side. The scar was
clean and straight, as if someone had run the blade of a
knife through it.

"We're here to pick up some horses for Jack

Stringer,'' Starky spoke up. ''We just come up from
the wood yard.''

''I know where you come from,'' he said gruffly.
''We've been watchin' you from back at camp all
evenin'.''

''We're in a hurry,'' said Gene. ''Stringer wants
those horses right away.''

''Is that so?'' he said, running his hand over his nose
again. ''A lot of people come around here wantin'
horses. That don't mean we should give them none.''

''If you'll let me get into my pocket,'' Starky said,
''I'll show you that we work for Stringer.''

''Do it slow.''

Starky pulled out his .50 Sharps shell. ''This came
from your pa. That is, if you're a Taggert.''

''I'm a Taggert,'' he said with a scoff. ''You damn
well better remember it, too.'' He urged his horse
ahead and leveled his rifle on Starky while he reached
down and took the shell. He looked at it a moment and
gave it back, asking, ''Where's Stringer?''

''He's back up on—'' Starky started.

''And why didn't Bull and LaFarge come up with
you from the wood yard?''

''Listen, Junior,'' Starky said with a growl. ''We
come a long ways to pick up some horses. Now we've
got no time to waste listening to you. It's your old man
we've got business with.''

''And I'm tired of my hands being up in the air like
this,'' Gene put in. ''If you want to shoot it out fine.
Just be ready to shoot it out again with Stringer when he
finds out about this.''

Taggert studied them all a moment while they put
their hands down, before he turned and motioned the
other two down off the hill. They were both as ragged
and dirty as their brother. One of them was good-sized

and looked to be in his middle twenties, though it was
hard to tell because of his slanting forehead and oversized lips. His eyes were dull looking and never focused on anything or anybody for very long. He had a
crop of light brown hair that poked out from under his
hat in all directions like the bristles on a hairbrush. He
seemed hardly concerned with anything that was going
on, but he made a funny sound in his throat when he
saw Janet. He wasn't doing much more than taking up
space.

The other one was entirely different. He was very
small in stature, with dark features and a set of searching black eyes that looked deep into a person and held
there. He was quiet, content to listen and form his
opinions for himself.

"These are two of my brothers," the split-nosed one
said. "You just remember that we're all Taggerts."

"I don't see your old man yet," Starky said. "I told
you once that I'm dealing with him, not a bunch of
smart-ass kids."

"He thinks he's pretty big, don't he?" the split-
nosed one said to the other two. "He called me Junior
just before you came down. Yeah, he thinks he's pretty
big stuff."

"It doesn't look to me like we'll get any horses from
here," Scott announced. "I say we just gun these
bastards down and ride on out."

"Now, don't get upset here," the split-nosed one
said after a moment's silence. "We was just havin' a
little fun, that's all."

"The fun's over," said Gene. "We want those
horses. *Now!*" He said it sharply, and all three
Taggerts jumped a little.

"Maybe they don't even have any horses," Scott
put in. "How do we even know they're who they say
they are?"

The split-nosed one turned to his small brother. "Show them who we are, Lit," he said.

The small one looked a little mad at having been called Lit in front of strangers. It was most likely a nickname for Little that he had been stuck with since childhood. He produced a rifle shell from his pocket and tossed it down to Gene, saying, "Now you tell me who's riding LaFarge's palomino."

"By God, that is LaFarge's horse," the split-nosed one observed.

Janet spoke up. "He and I made a trade until he gets back up here. He had something I wanted and . . . well, I had something for him."

Lit was silent, but the other two snickered.

Scott tossed the shell back to Lit. "So why aren't we looking at those horses yet?" he asked.

"It's gettin' too dark to deal horses," the split-nosed Taggert said. "We'll be back in the mornin' to get you. How's that sound?"

"Bring your old man," Starky said in a heavy tone.

"We'll see what he's got to say about this when we get back," the split-nosed one said. "This just ain't the way the deal was planned."

"Don't think we won't tell Stringer how we was treated over here," Starky was saying at the same time. "I don't give a damn about your plans. Your operation just don't stack up to what Stringer led us to believe. He's going to be mighty disappointed in what I've got to tell him."

The three Taggerts were silent. It appeared that they were convinced that Stringer had sent them after the horses. They were even beginning to feel apologetic about the whole thing. They were acting like they had done something wrong that hadn't been their fault.

"We'll be back for you tomorrow," the split-nosed one said. "It's just that Pa didn't—"

"Get the hell out of here," Starky broke in. "You'd damn well better be here by first light or we're gone. Them horses don't make any difference to us. It's Stringer that'll be hopping mad about this."

"Just don't leave," the split-nosed one said. "Just stay here. We'll be back tomorrow for sure."

The three Taggerts were gone, lost among the deep-cut coulees and the dark shadows of late evening. Gene and Janet walked to the top of the hill to watch the sunset. It was a big ball of crimson that spread its glow out across the sky and set the broken ridges of the badlands on fire. Soon the color had pulled itself down over the horizon and Scott was looking into the red embers of a campfire.

Starky was bending over a can of coffee. He filled his cup and went to his saddlebag, where he found a small harmonica. He made a backrest of his saddle and sat down to play.

Scott listened for a time while Starky held the little harp to his lips, pulling out a slow ballad that drifted softly through the camp and out into the night. It was a mournful tune that Scott had never heard, but he knew just by listening that the song was something special to Starky.

"What's the name of that tune, Starky?" he asked.

Starky sipped at his coffee. "It's a tune a young fiddler taught me just before Shiloh. He said his brother had written it. He called it "Sweet Lily, To-morrow."

"A Civil War tune?" Scott asked.

Starky nodded. "Yeah, he said his brother wrote it the night before they enlisted. I can still remember him telling me about it like it was yesterday. We were all sitting up on this big hill waiting for it to get light enough to shoot. We were all scared soldiers that night." He took another sip of coffee. "Dewey was his name. Dewey Culhane. I helped bury him and his fiddle the next day, just after noon.''

Starky went back into his song, and Scott looked out from the fire to see the figures of Gene and Janet as they stood talking next to her big palomino. They were no doubt discussing their lives and what lay ahead for them. Scott knew that by this time both of them had become interested in talking about how the future would look if it were shared together. The thought of what could happen tomorrow had to be wearing heavy on them. What if they were both killed? Or just one and not the other? What about *all* of them? Starky's song made it easy to see how they were just like soldiers before battle: the uncertainty, the fear and worry for those they loved, the sick and hollow feeling of knowing what was to come and not being able to do anything about it. There was nothing to do but wait.

Gene and Janet came back into camp and went over to the fire for some coffee. They filled their cups and settled down in the grass next to each other while Starky kept blowing ''Sweet Lily, Tomorrow.''

''That's so sad, Starky,'' Janet finally said. ''Play something more lively.''

Starky nodded and broke into an old fiddle tune called ''Arkansas Traveler,'' stomping his right boot against the ground for rhythm. Janet began clapping to the music and was soon joined by Gene and Scott. But Starky wasn't in the mood for an up-tempo tune, and he soon finished it.

The camp was quiet a moment before Gene said, ''You play that thing pretty good, Starky.''

He shrugged. ''Passes the time away. Helps a man out some when he's feeling low, too, I guess.''

''You're worried about tomorrow, aren't you?'' Gene said.

Starky came up off his saddle and seated himself

cross-legged. He slapped the harmonica against the palm of his hand a few times to get the moisture out. "I just don't like times like this," he said. "A man's got to face them, I know. These times come, and he just can't run away from them. Just the same, it's hard for an old codger like me who's seen it all before."

"What makes you more worried about going through the rest of this than the first part of it at the wood yard?" Scott asked.

"We're going into this part of it blind," Starky answered. "At the wood yard we had just Bull and LaFarge to worry about, and we had the jump on them to boot. We don't even know where we're at in here, and we don't even know for sure what's going to happen next. The only thing we know for sure is they're all killers who don't give a hoot or a holler for anything more than a few lousy dollars in their pockets. As it stands now, we've just got to hope Old Man Taggert feels that we're part of Stringer's bunch."

"Those three he sent down here seemed sure enough about it when they left," Gene said.

"That don't necessarily mean he will, though," Starky said, shaking his head. "Especially when he learns what we said about Bull and LaFarge being down at the wood yard. I'm afraid that's going to set him off some. And I'm afraid he won't want to deal any horses until they come back."

"We've got plenty of time to get those horses and get out before he learns what we did to those two," Gene said. "If he doesn't want to deal the horses, I guess we'll just have to shoot it out with them."

"That's what it's going to come down to, sure as hell," Starky said. "I thought maybe we could just ride in there and ride out without getting ourselves shot at, but I don't see how it can be done."

"Maybe we ought to plan on just taking them all the first chance we get," Gene suggested.

"I wish it were that easy," Starky said. "It's going to be hard to get the jump on them, and not knowing how many of them there are makes it that much tougher."

"There can't be that many of them left," Scott put in. "We got three at Powder River and two at the wood yard we know about for sure. Maybe somebody wounded one or two more somewhere along the line. The odds don't look that bad to me."

"We'll do it," Janet said. "We'll come out of this in good fashion."

"I didn't really want any of you to catch me fussing over it," Starky confessed. "It's just that you're about the best bunch of young folks that I ever met. As for me, one more day or one more year won't make a difference. But I'd sure hate to see anything happen to any of you. You're just a good bunch of people." He slapped the harmonica against his hand again. "I just wanted to say that in case I didn't get another chance."

Janet went over and sat down next to him. "I've never met anybody like you before, Starky. You are as good a man as God ever made. I want you to know that no matter what happens, I will always be grateful for this part of my life and how you helped me. No matter what happens to me, it will all have been worth it." The tears in her eyes glistened in the light of the fire, and a few spilled down her cheeks as she leaned over, kissed him, and gave him a hug.

"She spoke for me, too," Gene said.

"She spoke for all of us," Scott added. "We all feel the same way."

Janet went back over to Gene while Starky rubbed a wrinkled fist across his nose and sniffed quickly. "It's about time we all turned in,'' he said. ''We've got a lot of things we've got to get done tomorrow.''

The fire had died down to glowing embers by the time all the bedrolls had been filled. Somewhere off in the night a coyote's howl echoed, and nearby the crickets and the little spring puddle frogs once again took up their singing. Starky hadn't yet put away his harmonica, and he was blowing a few tunes before he went to sleep. He started out on ''Sweet Betsy from Pike'' and got through one verse before he changed to a waltz tune that Scott didn't know. After just two bars of the waltz, he dropped it and went into ''Sweet Lily, Tomorrow.''

Chapter 14

The same three Taggerts showed up again just after
sunup and led the way into the most well-hidden piece
of ground God ever dug in the face of the earth. It
seemed as if all that broken country had suddenly
smoothed out into a nice little grassy flat next to a big
spring of sparkling fresh water.

The flat was surrounded by walls of steep shale and
sandstone; it looked as if it had been built there instead
of just popping up on its own. The walls came together
into a narrow gorge where the thieves had fenced it off
with long poles fashioned into a gate. This was where
the only trail came into their domain from the outside
world. On the far side of the flat, the steep walls
tapered off into a pine-covered hillside that led to an
opening at the top of the cliffs. It served as a lookout
that took in country for miles around in every direction.
The trail up to the lookout had been roped off, and
makeshift poles and braces had been built up against
the bottom row of pines. The little flat was a perfect
oversized corral that furnished ample forage and water.

Just below the lookout, the thieves had built two
cabins—one appreciably larger than the other—and
had dug the spring out and rocked the sides to help keep

the water clear. Most of the horses were in this area, browsing casually for fresh spears of grass or working to keep the flies off. Scott saw with mixed relief and anxiety that a lot of them were branded with a Circle 6 and that none of the brands showed signs of having been tampered with.

Old Man Taggert was standing in front of the larger of the two cabins with his big Sharps rifle resting across his arms. He was a big man, outsizing all of his sons except the now-deceased Bull. He had once had the same dark features as his smallest son, Lit, but now they were heavily streaked with gray, especially the tangled mat of patchy beard. What he still shared with Lit was a set of cold, piercing eyes.

He was flanked by a husky young blond, alert and very perceptive. He was the youngest of the Taggerts and seemed to be a mixture of meanness and intelligence. He stood casually listening to what was being said and, like his brother Lit, was turning it all over in his mind and sorting through it for loopholes.

Old Man Taggert let his split-nosed son repeat what Starky had been saying about getting rid of all stolen horses because of vigilante actions in the country before he asked Starky for the whole story. Starky went through the same procedure he had used on Bull and LaFarge at the wood yard. Judging by Taggert's responses, he seemed to be going along with everything he was hearing. But he was still very much on edge about not having Bull and LaFarge there, too.

"They told us they hadn't seen Crazy Alice and her girls for a long spell and wanted to celebrate some," Starky told him. "Scully said you'd spot us easy once we got up in this country. This map made it pretty simple for us."

Taggert took the map while he shook his head. "I can't figure why they'd do that. They both know this business comes first and that they'll have all the time they want down there as soon as this thing is finished."

Starky tried to smooth it over a bit. "They didn't say for sure, but no doubt they'll be along later today or early tomorrow. They just wanted a little fun. Can't blame them for that."

Taggert put the map in his pocket and looked over to where the horses were all gathered near the water. "Fun, hell! I sent them two down there to pick up a fella that was supposed to come up here and work the brands over on these horses. I can't figure why they didn't send him up here with you if they weren't comin'. You see anybody else down there?"

Starky shook his head. "We didn't see nobody else. But it don't matter none; we've got people who can work on brands themselves. The way I see it, you can't hardly wait on getting them all changed now, anyway, being things are like they are with the ranchers in the country."

Old Man Taggert thought a moment. "Would you be willing to pay the same money that we agreed to begin with?"

Starky frowned. "There's more horses here than Stringer told us he bargained for. He gave us enough to cover forty head, tops. Being that the brands aren't changed, he wouldn't want us to give top money."

"Now, see? That's the whole damn thing!" Taggert exploded. "Them two know we've got to have the brands worked over before we sell to make any money. Them two are really gonna be sorry, I swear to God!"

His sons were silent. Scott thought back on what the kid at the Powder River had said about Old Man Taggert and his temper. Taggert was only half mad now, since he was among strangers he didn't know quite what to make of. It was hard to imagine what kind of rage he exhibited when he was being himself.

Taggert cooled off and looked hard at Janet and her palomino. "That's a little hard to figure, too," he said. "Lit said last night that you were ridin' LaFarge's horse as a swap for some whorin' with you. That right?"

Janet's eyes widened with the remark. "I can see that your vocabulary is limited to vulgarities," she told him. "Let's just call it an agreement. I only get the horse until he makes it back up here or we leave, whichever comes first."

"That sure seems funny to me," Taggert went on. "He gave up two months' pay for that horse. There wasn't nothin' that could separate him from the damn thing."

"A woman has her ways," Janet pointed out.

"LaFarge has got a woman," Taggert came back. "Some bitch down at the wood yard. Didn't she have no say about it?"

"Crazy Alice told her to get back into bed and wait until she was told to get up," Janet informed him. "I don't have to sleep in the daytime."

Taggert grunted and headed inside the bigger of the two cabins. Scott and Janet went inside behind Taggert's sons, and Gene stayed in the doorway, playing his role as lookout and gunman well.

The bigger cabin was where the thieves slept. It was lined with bunks, and the only table in the room was covered with stolen guns and other loot from the various raids they had been on. The other cabin served as their cooking house and supply shed. Taggert had brought them into the bunkhouse so that he wouldn't have to worry about them seeing anything but musty bedcovers and plain log walls. He was nervous enough about having them in his horse ranch at all.

Starky talked about getting down to business with the horses, but Taggert wanted to hold off until Bull and LaFarge got back, just as Starky had feared. They argued back and forth for the better part of an hour, and Starky finally told him that they would wait a few more hours and that was all.

Taggert had gotten to the point where he wouldn't have cared if they had ridden out without taking the horses. Starky had felt it would be best to give him a little time to think what could happen if a bunch of stranglers caught them with all those stolen horses. As Starky kept bringing up the subject, it was plain that Taggert was beginning to think more and more about losing his neck if he didn't use his head.

As the evening wore on, Scott got more jittery. It wouldn't be long now until they would have to spend the night here and take the horses out in the morning. Time was their worst enemy now, and the more of it that passed, the harder it would be to get the horses. The thought of it didn't sit well, but Starky was playing it cool and waiting for the right moment to act.

Taggert spent most of his time rolling Bull Durham cigarettes and puffing on them while he paced the floor and made numerous trips to a big pocket watch he kept hanging on the wall next to his bunk. Scott had noticed that Gene had given it more than one look since Taggert's first trip and that a glint of anger had been showing in his eyes ever since. Whether it was the watch or Taggert himself that had set Gene off was hard to tell, but it was a fact that Starky was going to have to try to talk Taggert into doing business before very long or Gene was going to try to make the thieves a family of dead men.

Taggert and his sons all seemed to feel the same way. They drummed on the log walls with their fingers and joined in with their pa in chain-smoking cigarettes to ease the tension, but their faces showed worry. They all seemed to feel that Gene had the same job with

Starky and Jack Stringer's bunch that LaFarge did with them. It made them all nervous to think that there was a man of LaFarge's nature around who could easily be as deadly with a gun and that he wasn't on their side.

Old Man Taggert thought on it a while longer, at the same time hoping that Bull and LaFarge would come up the little flat and solve all their problems.

Taggert ground a cigarette into the dirt floor of the cabin and gave Gene a quick look before he turned to Starky. "I guess Bull and LaFarge ain't gonna make it back tonight. Maybe we'd better go look at those horses now if you'd like."

Starky seemed pleased and somehow puzzled at Taggert's sudden change of tune. Taggert agreed that getting rid of the horses would be in his best interest since the country was filling up with stranglers and regulators. As they started out from the cabin toward the horses, Taggert took a moment to talk to a couple of his sons in private. Scott's skin began to crawl. Maybe it didn't mean anything, but maybe it did.

They got to the spring and looked at a few horses while Taggert explained to Starky how hard it was to get them and where to go with them to avoid going back through the owners' country. All the while there was an eerie feeling that something wasn't right. Suddenly Janet yelped as one of the thieves grabbed her around the throat from behind and put his gun to her head.

It was the split-nosed son, and he had an evil grin on his face. His brothers all pulled their pistols, too, and Old Man Taggert moved back with his .50 Sharps rifle resting across his arms.

"I ain't figured how you got hold of one of my rifle shells yet," he told Starky. "But one thing I am sure of: You sure as hell don't ride for Jack Stringer. Bring them back inside, boys."

Scott moved forward with the bristly-haired Taggert's Colt jammed into his back. His brother with the split nose had released Janet and was paying particular attention to her. He was walking as close as he could to her and was looking around at the others as if he had just found a twenty-dollar gold piece and was laying claim to it. His mouth was drawn back across his uneven yellow teeth, and he could hardly keep from grabbing her again.

"What the hell is this all about?" Starky was saying at the same time. "By God, I can't figure this out for—"

"Cut the playactin'," Old Man Taggert broke in. "You put on a good show there for a while, but I ain't buyin' it, not no more. Like I said, that rifle shell of mine that you've got has me stumped, and I can't figure how you buffaloed Bull and LaFarge like you did, but I know you ain't with Stringer now."

Scott's stomach cramped up tight. There was no use pretending anymore. Taggert somehow knew what they were up to. It was a good bet that he didn't yet know that his giant son and LaFarge wouldn't be coming back, though; otherwise, he would have killed all four of them by now. The question at this time was: how long would it be until he got worried enough to send one of his other boys down to the wood yard to check up on them? Scott had his answer as soon as they were inside the cabin.

A black feeling of doom settled over him as he noticed that the youngest Taggert was gone and heard the sound of a horse outside at the same time. The young blond stuck his head in the door as he prepared to leave.

"Anythin' else, Pa?" he asked.

Old Man Taggert gave him the map he had gotten from Starky. "Find out about this from Scully, too," he said. "Tell that stupid bastard never to draw any more maps for nobody. And make sure he understands."

"He'll be back with Bull and LaFarge before daybreak," Old Man Taggert told Starky as he watched his son leave. "Until then, we'll just sit tight here and wait for them."

"What makes you think we don't ride with Stringer?" Gene questioned him.

Taggert had a smirk on his face. "Well, for one thing, your name is Huntley. Ain't that right?"

Gene tried to hide his surprise, but his eyes widened a bit.

"Yeah, sure it is," Taggert said with a laugh. "You're Gene Huntley sure as hell."

Then the bristly-haired son came into the cabin, his eyes glowing and his mouth in a grin from ear to ear. He was holding up a large white flour sack that had been sewn to fit over a man's head and shoulders, with cuts for the arms and two holes in the top for eyes.

"Look at what I found in one of those saddlebags, Pa," he said. "Ain't this somethin' to see?"

There was silence in the cabin. Scott's eyes were large as they went from the flour sack to Gene and then to Starky. Gene's face held no expression, and Starky looked to the floor.

Old Man Taggert laughed. "How about that. We not only got ourselves Gene Huntley, but we also got the White Bandit!"

Chapter 15

The bristly-haired Taggert laughed and pulled the flour sack down over his head and danced around the room. He whooped and hollered and then pretended he was sneaking around like a ghost. His split-nosed brother laughed wickedly and goaded him on, while Lit and the young blond one looked on stoically.

Finally Old Man Taggert tired of the entertainment and yelled out that the fun was over. His bristly-haired son continued to yell and dance around, his mind occupied only with what he was doing.

"I said stop," Old Man Taggert blared. He cuffed his son in the middle of the back with the butt of his Sharps rifle.

The bristly-haired son let out a deep groan and staggered into the wall, holding his back. Then he began struggling to free himself from the flour sack while Old Man Taggert cuffed him again with the rifle butt. Finally Taggert set the rifle down and, with heated disgust, jerked the sack off his son, leaving him in a sprawled heap on the floor.

"You idiot," he bellowed. "Can't you listen to nothin' I tell you? Just once?"

"I was just funnin', Pa. That's all."

"Get up!"

"Pa, don't be mad. I'm sorry."

"I said get up!" Taggert bellowed louder. "And quit whinin' like some poor puppy dog or somethin'. You make me sick!" He watched his son climb to his feet, and then he ordered him, "Now help the others tie them all up. And fast!"

"Hey, wait, Pa," the split-nosed son said quickly. He was breathing a bit unevenly, and his eyes were riveted on Janet as he spoke. "We can't tie somethin' this pretty up like that. Looks to me like that would sure be a waste. Besides, I'd kind of like to find out what's so special about her that LaFarge would give up that horse."

The bristly-haired Taggert agreed with him, and their small brother, Lit, remained, as usual, reserved and quiet.

Janet seemed to be expecting the whole thing and began to act aggressively toward them. "I was beginning to wonder if you boys cared at all about a woman," she said, as if she was flattered by their attention. She was playing her role well, and it seemed to stimulate the two Taggerts even more. "Just so you all have enough to spend to make it worth my while."

The bristly-haired one shrugged as if it didn't matter to him. The son with the split nose edged as close as he could to her while she made coy moves to get away from him.

Lit watched her with narrowed eyes. "You boys are goin' for a ride with her," he warned. "If it was me, I wouldn't pay her a damned thing. In fact, she's goin' to have me for nothin'."

Janet looked down her nose at him. "That's fine. Just don't expect a very good time. And you'll have to wait until last."

The other two jeered their small brother and sided with Janet. He told them again how he thought they were fools, but their laughing and joking about how Janet had put him down drowned out anything he had to say. They couldn't have cared less what he thought, anyway.

The split-nosed Taggert produced a roll of bills from his pocket and asked, "Will this be enough?"

Janet took the money like a professional and gave him a look that nearly drove him wild. His bristly-haired brother wanted in on the act, too, and so he reached down into his own pocket.

"Hey, I got money, too," he called out.

The split-nosed one gave him a shove and said, "You just back off and wait your turn. Hear?"

"That ain't fair, Zeke," he protested. "Who said you could be first?"

"Hold on here," Old Man Taggert bellowed. "You ain't about to start fightin' over no woman now!"

"Calm down, Daddy," Janet said with a cute smile. "I'll just take both of them with me, and nobody will be upset. I thought we'd just take a little moonlight stroll up to that lookout. There must be a nice grassy spot somewhere up there."

Lit shook his head and spoke up while his two brothers whooped and hollered at the idea. "Why don't you go up there with her just one at a time maybe," he advised them. "Flip a coin or somethin' to see who goes first."

"You stay out of this, Lit," said his split-nosed brother. "We'll settle that between us once we get up there. Where do you get off thinkin' you got any say in this, anyway, since you're too damn cheap to pay the lady what she's worth."

"Yeah, Lit. He's right," the bristly-haired son

echoed, and joined his brother in laughter as the two of them ushered Janet out the door.

"You don't stay up there too long now, hear?" Old Man Taggert yelled after them. "We ain't on no lark here, you know."

"I don't like it, Pa," Lit said.

"I'd rather the two of them go together than alone," the old man said.

"Yeah, but why do they have to go clear up there?" Lit wanted to know. "What the hell's wrong with down here?"

"Just tie these other three up and let me worry about the rest of it," Old Man Taggert ordered; he didn't want his authority questioned.

Lit shook his head again as he took some ropes from the gear piled on the table.

"I thought I'd seen you before," Old Man Taggert was saying while Lit set to work tying Gene's hands. "When I caught you lookin' at my watch earlier, I remembered then that you were kin to those hide hunters we got it from down in the Black Hills."

"How did you know that?" Gene asked. "You've never seen me before to know me."

"Oh, yes, I have. You just about caught up to us in that Belle Fouche saloon down there. Remember? If that saloonkeeper hadn't tipped us off who you were when you got off your horse outside, you might have come in there and got the drop on us."

Gene shook his head in anger as he thought back on the incident. "I knew that saloonkeeper was lying to me about you not being there. I should have shot the son of a bitch."

"We was in the back room all the time." Taggert laughed. "Now I guess we'll have to show you what we did to your kin."

Lit pushed them down into a sitting position with their backs against the wall. He studied Gene for a moment, stretching himself as high as he could go without rising on his tiptoes. His complex about being small was showing itself fully now, and he was taking advantage of Gene's inferior position on the floor.

"I knew you were all a bunch of phonies," he said, smirking. "I knew it right off the bat. Now you'll get a chance to join your kinfolk in hell." He snorted. "The White Bandit. Ha!"

Gene's eyes narrowed. "You're not big enough to scare anybody, even when you've got them tied up."

Lit gave him a swift kick to the side of the head. Gene was momentarily dazed, but the blow had struck him high enough not to do much harm.

"I ought to kick your teeth out," Lit shouted. "But we'll take them out like we did with those lousy hide hunters you called family." His mouth broke into a wicked grin. "They sure had a lot of gold in their mouths. We got it all out, too."

Old Man Taggert started laughing again and decided to come over by his small son. He squatted down with a rifle in Gene's face. "Open up," he ordered.

Gene glared at him.

"I said open up," he bellowed as he jammed the muzzle of the rifle into Gene's mouth viciously, splitting his lower lip. "You do what I say, hear?"

He grabbed Gene's face and roughly squeezed his cheeks together so that Gene's mouth was forced open. Blood from the cut lip was dripping out into the palm of his hand. "I don't see any gold in your mouth, though," he said as he moved Gene's head roughly and peered into his mouth. "Maybe we'll have to take them out, anyway." He laughed treacherously and wiped the blood from his hand.

"How about gramps there?" Lit said, pointing down to Starky. "His mouth ought to be plumb full of gold."

Old Man Taggert turned his eyes to Starky. "How about it?" he demanded.

Starky shook his head with cold, unafraid eyes.

"You wouldn't be fibbin' us, now, would you?" he growled. He pinched Starky's jaws open in the same manner he had Gene's. After putting his rifle down, he stuck a dirt-blackened finger inside Starky's mouth and began pushing his cheeks out to look in the back. Finally he quit and got up with a grunt. "I don't suppose you do, either," he said to Scott.

"No, I don't," Scott said.

"I guess they don't got any dentists in this part of the country, eh?" Taggert said with disgust. He looked back to Gene. "We got about half rich on those kin of yours down there." He laughed. "Gold or no gold, I'll bet you squeal just as loud as they did." Still laughing, he picked a half-full bottle of whiskey from the floor near his bunk and set to work on it.

Scott watched Gene sitting next to him with his head down, helplessly mad and torn apart at the memory of his brothers and what the Taggerts had done to them. His bruised lip was swelling badly, and a dark blue color was invading the flesh on his lower chin.

Looking to Starky, it was easy to see how bad he felt. What the Taggerts had planned for them seemed secondary to their empathy for Gene. They could see why six years hadn't subdued his feeling of hate for the gang of thieves. Another thing that troubled all three of them just as much was Janet. Scott felt sick at the thought of what was happening to her at the lookout. Then the door opened, and the bristly-haired son stuck his head inside.

''Pa, get out here,'' he screamed. ''The other cabin's on fire!'' He pulled his head back and left the door slightly ajar.

Old Man Taggert got a puzzled look on his face. The faint smell of smoke was in the air and seemed to be getting stronger. Lit's eyes widened with suspicion, and he drew his pistol.

The bristly-haired son started yelling about bringing pails to get water from the spring. The smoke smell was getting pretty strong, and both Old Man Taggert and Lit were beginning to get worried.

''You keep an eye on them, Lit,'' Old Man Taggert ordered. ''I'd better see what the hell's goin' on out there.''

Lit was saying, ''Pa, call Zeke in here first. Wait!'' But he couldn't stop him in time. He was just going through the door when the muzzle of a Colt .45 appeared in his face.

''It was a short trip to Lover's Lookout,'' Janet said.

Chapter 16

The smell of smoke was heavy and the sound of cracking wood grew louder as Janet backed Old Man Taggert and herded his bristly-haired son through the door. "Order that sawed-off son of yours there to drop his gun," she told Taggert.

Old Man Taggert said nothing, and Lit kept his gun trained toward Gene.

"How would you like this thing to go off in your face, Taggert?" Janet asked gruffly. "I want to hear that gun drop. Now!"

Lit cursed, and his pistol thudded to the dirt floor of the cabin. Janet lined all three of them up against a wall while Scott, Gene, and Starky helped each other out of the ropes.

"I could have predicted that you'd manage to get away if there had been just one to contend with," Starky said, laughing. "But what in the world did you come up with to handle both of them?"

Janet said, "If you kick a man where it counts, then roll him off a cliff, he can't do much to you."

"You've got a point there," Starky said. "Then you decided you'd celebrate with a bonfire."

Janet laughed. "That dried pine burns real well. I'm

afraid our little fire won't last too long.''

Old Man Taggert's eyes were filled with rage. He looked at his bristly-haired son, who stood next to him with his hands in the air and a glazed expression on his face. ''What's the matter with you? Where's Zeke?''

Janet spoke for him. ''He's at the bottom of that lookout, right where he belongs.''

''Is he dead?''

''He couldn't have fallen that far and still be alive.''

Taggert stiffened, and his lips curled back. ''You did that?'' he hissed.

''If I were you, I'd just relax,'' Janet advised him. ''After putting up with those two animals all the way up that hill, my trigger finger is pretty jerky.''

''Ah, you wouldn't shoot that thing,'' Taggert said, challenging her. ''You ain't got the guts for it.'' He started toward her.

Janet shoved the muzzle of the Colt hard into Taggert's throat, bringing a gagging sound from him as his head went back. ''Just try me. I don't need much of an excuse.''

Taggert backed up and turned his wrath on his bristly-haired son. ''Where the hell were you all the time?''

''Zeke was supposed to have her first.'' He shrugged. ''I don't know . . .''

Old Man Taggert shook his head in disgust. ''So then you come down here and just watch while she burns the cooking house and stick your head in the door as big as you please and lead me out into a trap.''

''I couldn't help it, Pa,'' he said weakly. ''She was ready to blow my head off, just like now.''

''Is what she said about Zeke bein' dead true?''

His son answered blankly as if hoping he was in a dream. ''I don't know, Pa. She went into the trees with

him, and the next thing I know, she's got his .45
planted in my belly and I hear him screamin'. I don't
know, Pa. It just happened so quick."

Old Man Taggert cursed and got a look on his face
like he was finally beginning to realize that he was no
longer in charge but a captive. Lit stood silent and
dark-faced. It wasn't hard to see that he was boiling
mad at himself for going along with something he
knew was bound to end up getting them in trouble.

Janet asked Gene about his split lip while Scott and
Starky got the last of the ropes off each other.

Gene went over, rubbing the numbness out of his
wrists. "That came courtesy of this son of a bitch," he
said, glaring at Old Man Taggert. "I aim to return the
favor."

Taggert leaned back into the wall as if expecting a
blow.

Gene smiled wryly. "No, it won't be right now. I
want you to have some time to think about it."

"You'd better get your best shot in now," Taggert
growled. "When Bull and LaFarge get back, it'll be all
over for you."

Gene played along, not telling him about the wood
yard gunfight. "Oh, I don't know," he said. "Bull and
LaFarge weren't too hot about leavin' down there. I
think Bull's planning on marrying Crazy Alice."

"What the hell do you know about it?" Taggert
asked.

Gene laughed. "They're just two pigs in a puddle,
and I don't know which one is uglier."

Old Man Taggert's eyes blazed. He acted like he
wanted to take a swing at Gene but had thought better
of it.

Lit spoke up, his eyes full of hate. "It's pretty easy
to talk that way to an older man," he said.

Gene walked over to the middle of the room. "I'm

not tied up anymore, you little bastard," he said evenly. "Put your hands down and come over here if you've got any more to say. Otherwise, shut your little bitty face."

Lit should have known better than to challenge Gene, as mad as he was. But Lit was hot too. Then his sudden burst of anger turned to clearer thinking, and he began to wonder whether he had been using his head very well when he had spoken. He decided he would look for an out.

"Hell," he said. "As soon as I get the best of you, the others will shoot me."

"Our guns don't shoot half bullets," Gene retorted. "It would be a waste of lead to use a whole bullet on you."

Lit licked his lips and doubled his fists. He had dealt the cards, and Gene had called his bluff; now he was going to have to play the hand as best he could. The more he stared into Gene's dark face, the shakier he got. Gene was a good ten inches taller and probably outweighed him by forty pounds. It was too late to measure size now, and Lit knew he had been talking when he should have been listening.

"Are you comin' over here or not?" Gene prodded him. "We haven't got any dolls for you to play with."

Lit bolstered his courage with a deep breath and took his hat off. He rushed at Gene in one quick movement, hoping to catch him off guard. But Gene was waiting for him. He caught Lit by the hair and jerked his head back violently, exposing his face to a crushing blow that brought the crunch of shattering teeth and bone along with a withered moan from Lit that died out when he hit the floor. Lit lay motionless in a sprawled heap, with the left side of his face caved in and a pool of blood forming around his head.

"I thought he had more brains than to tackle Gene,"

Starky said under his breath. "They might as well bury him now."

Old Man Taggert and his bristly-haired son were stone silent. Their faces went from shock to cold fear.

Gene knelt down, turned Lit's broken face up to the light, and worked open the bloody mouth. He reached in and found a piece of broken tooth. "I don't see any gold in that one," he said, holding it up for Old Man Taggert to see. "But he's got more in there, and I'll bet some of them do." He looked up to where Lit's bristly-haired brother was standing. "How about you? How much gold is in your mouth?"

He turned chalk white. "No . . . I ain't . . . I ain't never been to . . . to no dentist."

"You sure?"

"No, I swear. Really, I ain't."

Gene threw the tooth across the room and stood up. He went over to Old Man Taggert with his fist doubled in front of him. "I think I owe you one of these, too," he said coldly. "My lip don't feel too good because of you, but I've got it figured that you'll feel a lot worse than I do when I'm through."

Taggert was trying to act bold, but he was deathly afraid of Gene. "You've been forgettin' about Bull and LaFarge," he said. "They ain't goin' to be one bit happy when they see what's happened here."

"I'm not too worried about them," Gene told him.

"They won't just ride down in here straight out, not after seein' how the cooking house is burned," Taggert went on. "They ain't that dumb."

"That doesn't matter to us," Gene told him. "We'll be long gone with the horses by then, and you and this other bastard of yours will be swinging from a big yellow pine."

Taggert was seething with anger. "How the hell do

you expect to get anywhere with them horses? You can't travel now; you can't go anywhere until it gets light."

"I think we can manage," Gene told him.

Taggert was confident. "Not hardly," he argued. "Just think about it. Them gumbo knobs all look the same, and to somebody who's only seen them once before, it can be damn hard to get your bearings straight. When you consider that you've got a night with no moon, your chances go plumb to hell."

"Maybe we'll have you lead us out," Gene suggested.

Taggert shook his head. "Not a chance."

"Don't you care whether you live or die?" Gene asked.

"That don't scare me none," Taggert said with a shake of his head. "It's blacker than hell out there right now. You can do anything you want to us, and it still won't get those horses out of these badlands for you. If you wait around here much longer, you'll have to answer to Bull and LaFarge. But we already talked about that, now, didn't we?" His mouth was curled back in an ugly grin.

"Too bad you're so damned sure of things around here," Gene said. "A while back you thought you'd done something pretty smart by catching us. Now, thanks to your half-wit son, all you've got to look forward to is a rope around your worthless neck."

Taggert was so mad, he was shaking. "You ain't about to kill us, not if you're smart. You can talk all you want, but you know that any way you look at it, you ain't about to get out of here without my say-so, not and take any horses with you. There's no way you can get out of these badlands with a bunch of horses in the dark, not even if you knew the country as well as we do. Sure, you could get rid of us and hightail it right now without the horses and maybe find your way out, but then you wouldn't want to come all this way and not have any horses to show for it, now, would you?'' He was grinning as if he thought he had Gene in a corner. ''And if you wait until it gets light, Bull and LaFarge will be back here for sure.''

Gene was trying to keep from laughing. ''You've really got us over a barrel, don't you?''

''Like I said, if you want those horses, you'll need my say-so on it. You might kill us, but you won't get out of here then. They'll pick you all off like flies once you try goin' out of that gate at the far end. I was thinkin' that maybe we could make some kind of deal.''

What Taggert had said about trying to take the horses out of there in the dark was true. That would be foolish to try if they didn't want to scatter the herd all over the badlands and risk serious injury to the horses and themselves in the process. Old Man Taggert was using his head in good fashion there, but he had no way of knowing that using Bull and LaFarge to get him out of his predicament was useless. Since they were planning on waiting until daylight to move the horses anyway, Gene decided to carry on with his little game.

''What kind of deal were you thinking about?'' he asked.

Taggert broke into a grin. ''Well, we're no good to you dead; you know that. Maybe you could swap us to Bull and LaFarge for your horses and a safe trip out of here.''

Gene was enjoying the game. ''Well, maybe that's the best we can hope for.''

Taggert was grinning broadly now as if he had things under full control. ''I know it's the best you can hope for," he said. "I'd consider myself lucky if I were you."

Scott and Gene tied Old Man Taggert and his bristly-haired son and left them struggling from the same sitting position against the wall that they themselves had been in a short time before. Lit still hadn't moved since Gene's punch had felled him, and so Gene grabbed him by the hair and pulled him out of the middle of the room. Taggert seemed fairly content thinking that his huge son, Bull, and the killer, LaFarge, would appear almost any time and that things would be settled in their favor. There wasn't much point wasting time trying to tell them any different. Taggert would just feel that it was a ploy to make them forget about any deals for their lives, and he wouldn't believe anything anyone might tell him about his son being dead.

The four of them moved just outside the door to iron out the escape they would make with the horses as soon as the light permitted. The cabin was now just a pile of charred wood and glowing coals; it was still smoking heavily. The immediate danger was that the youngest Taggert might return ahead of schedule with the men Jack Stringer had sent down from the Missouri. If they had shown up even four or five hours early at the wood yard, there was a better than even chance that they might ride in at almost any time.

"Taggert won't be wrong about having us in a spot if the others come riding in here on us," said Starky. "We've got to be out of here at first light."

"Do you think that young Taggert had enough sense to wait for Stringer's bunch?" Gene asked. "Maybe he's on his way back alone."

"I doubt it," said Starky. "He seemed to me like the type that can keep his head and use it when he has to.

That's why Taggert sent him down there instead of one of the others.''

"That means we'll have to take the horses south,'' Scott said.

"That's right,'' Starky concurred. "We can't take a chance on running into a whole bunch of them, especially when we don't have any idea how many of them to expect. If we go north, we take that chance.''

"My God,'' Janet whispered. "That country south looks a whole lot worse than what we rode into getting here from the north.''

"It is worse, but we can't help it,'' Starky said. "We'll just have to hope that we can find a series of coulees that lead us down to the Yellowstone somehow.''

"That's going to be a big somehow, '' Gene put in.

They went back inside to wait out the rest of the night. Lit still hadn't moved at all, and so Starky knelt down to check him. He thumbed one of Lit's eyelids back and found it dull and glazed over.

"This one's dead for sure,'' Starky told them all.

"I couldn't have hit him that hard,'' said Gene.

"There's a good chance you broke his neck when you hit him so hard, and his neck being twisted back like it was at the time,'' Starky speculated. "He went down awful loose. I thought at the time that he was most likely done for.''

Taggert wouldn't believe it. He kept on about how they were just trying to make him jumpy. Gene took Lit's dead body and dragged it over by Old Man Taggert. He propped it up against a bunk directly in front of the man and pulled open the glassy, unseeing eyes. He held Lit's head erect by the hair and said, "You two just take a good look at him for a while and decide for yourselves.'' He left the head leaning back against the bunk for them to see.

Janet turned away and started to gag.

"I guess he's not too pretty at that," Gene remarked. He gave the body a push with his boot, and it flopped over sideways into Old Man Taggert's lap. Taggert could only stare, dumbfounded.

"Convinced?" Gene asked, and pulled the body over to the side again.

Gene toyed with Old Man Taggert the rest of the night. He kept saying that he thought he heard riders. Then, when Taggert would perk up, he would announce that there was nobody there and that he must have been mistaken. Taggert held on to the false hope that Bull and LaFarge were indeed out there somewhere and were just waiting for the right opportunity to come in. But as the sky in the east took on a faint hint of gray, Taggert's confidence turned into concern. When the gray turned to pink, he became almost frantic.

Janet had been at the doorway most of the night, and as soon as she could make out where she was going, she was out saddling her horse. Scott and Starky both got ready to go help her while Gene volunteered to stay and watch the Taggerts. On the way out, Starky stopped in the doorway.

"They'll have to go back with us, Gene," he said. "They're entitled to a fair trial. That's the law."

"Don't you worry none about the law, Starky," Gene said with a sudden coldness in his voice. "I've got a special going-away party planned for these two."

Chapter 17

When Scott had finished saddling his buckskin, he followed Starky and Janet inside to let Gene know that they were ready to go. They found him putting the last knots in a rope that had Old Man Taggert hog-tied over the top of a narrow bunk bed. Gene had run the rope underneath the bunk and had tied Taggert's arms and legs to each other, leaving him facing up with his arms drawn back over the edge of the bed and his back arched uncomfortably.

Gene looked up and saw the three of them watching him curiously from the doorway. "Janet, maybe you'd best wait outside," he told her. "This won't be too pretty."

"Gene, what are you going to do?" she asked, moving forward.

"It doesn't concern you, Janet," was his answer. "This is a family matter that has been hanging fire for a lot of years."

Janet was troubled. "Hang them, yes, Gene, I can see that. But don't stoop to their level of torture."

Gene wasn't talking. Starky talked Janet into going outside with her horse while he talked to Gene. He brought Gene over to the doorway and began in a low tone.

"I don't know what you've got planned for sure, Gene, but don't go through with it."

Gene's eyes burned into Taggert for a moment before he spoke. "Look, Starky, that man's face has been eating at my memory ever since that day six years ago when my uncle led me out and showed me my slaughtered brothers. He butchered them all like animals!"

"Nothing you can do to him will bring them back, Gene."

"I don't expect it to, Starky. I just want to get this hate out of my system."

Starky shook his head. "I guess you weren't listening too close to what Janet was trying to tell you back at the wood yard after you gunned LaFarge down. Killing gets etched into your mind and takes over your life. Carving these Taggerts up won't rid you of your hate; you'll just do the same thing all over again to somebody else who makes you mad."

"I don't think so," Gene said, unmoved. "I don't feel this way toward anybody else but these bastards."

Starky shuffled his feet. "Well, if you won't forget it for your own sake, at least consider Janet. She means more to you than these two, doesn't she?"

Gene rubbed his brow to ease his tension. "Yes, Starky, she means a lot to me. But you see, my kin meant a lot to me, too." He breathed deeply and pointed over to the Taggerts. "And I can't forget what they did to them just for fun, either."

"I suppose chopping them all up will make you forget, huh?"

"Starky, I don't suppose *anything* will make me forget that."

"Something like this will only make those memories worse," Starky told Gene. "We'll take them back with us, and they'll stand trial."

"Starky, there's a chance they'll go free that way."

"No, no," Starky argued. "Not with these horses as evidence. You'll see them hang, and that's the right way to do it."

Gene turned and looked at the Taggerts. Old Man Taggert was grinning as if nobody in the world could ever hurt him.

"Forget it," Starky advised him again. "Let Scott here help you tie them to a couple of horses. I'll help Janet round up the rest of the herd."

Starky went out, and Gene continued to think on it as he watched the Taggerts and their wicked smiles. After a moment he said to Scott, "Maybe Starky has the right idea. They'll be just as dead at the end of a rope."

Gene told Scott to watch the Taggerts closely while he saddled horses for all of them. It wouldn't be easy taking the outlaws down the trail out of Makoshika with them, but it was the only way to stay within the law.

Scott held Gene's Winchester steady while the two Taggerts said everything they could think of to scare him into freeing them. When the scare tactics failed, there were offers of money and security in their gang of thieves if he would untie them. Scott said nothing the whole time.

When Gene came back, Old Man Taggert broke into a mocking laugh. "I don't know what the hell you think you're goin' to do with us," he said. "But you'd just as well let us go. You know you can't get away with takin' us out of here. Maybe you'd like to die like a dog, just the way your brothers did." He broke into a loud laugh, and his bristly-haired son joined in.

Gene shot cold eyes over at the two men, who were now laughing hysterically. Scott knew they had made a big mistake. Gene's face turned red with hatred, and he sucked in a mouthful of air. He yelled at the two Taggerts and pointed to the crushed and dead heap of humanity in the corner that was Lit, walking toward them as he spoke.

"You'll both wish you were him before I get through," he told them in a tone as hard as steel.

They both looked into the stony grayness of Lit's dead face, and the laughing died out instantly.

"You don't have to stay for this," Gene told Scott.

"We can't take a chance on one or both of them getting loose," Scott said. "I'll stick around."

Gene moved over to the bed where Old Man Taggert was tied. He leaned over and looked down into the outlaw's face with a burning glare. "Ever been to a dentist yourself?" he asked. When Taggert didn't answer, he straightened up and added, "I guess it really doesn't matter whether you have or not."

Gene walked over to the table where the Taggerts had piled their stolen guns and other loot. After probing around, he came up with a bone-handled skinning knife. He chucked the knife into the top of the table a few times and smiled.

"You're pretty good at finding gold in people's teeth," he told Taggert as he went back to the bed. "I'm not that good at just looking around in someone's open mouth and finding it. I have to take the teeth out one by one so I can look them over good."

Old Man Taggert got a horrified look on his face as Gene tested the sharpness of the knife against his thumb. He struggled frantically to pull loose from the ropes, but he looked like a fly trying to work his way out of a jar of honey. There was no doubt he was wishing he was someone other than Old Man Taggert.

Outside, the sky was turning from gray to light blue in the east, and the sounds of horses whinnying back and forth out near the spring could be heard. "I'll bet you wish you'd never seen a horse before in your life, don't you? And it's too bad you took such an interest in the hide business when you did." Gene was talking through a sinister grin. "But it's too late for all that now."

Taggert quit thrashing for a moment to catch his breath. His eyes were white with terror, and big beads of sweat were collecting on his forehead and wetting his beard along the mouth and upper chin. His bristly-haired son broke into sobs and begged Gene not to hurt him or his pa. Gene walked over and gave him a sharp kick to the ribs, bringing a squeal of pain and fright.

"Don't tell me you never did this, and worse, to other folks," Gene hissed. "You slobbering baby! It's high time you found out what it's like to see things from the other side for a change."

Young Taggert's bristly hair was matted from sweat, and his eyes rolled wide with fear. He held his breath a moment, afraid that his loud breathing would invoke another blow from Gene's boot.

"Now, I've got to get to work on your pa here," Gene told him with a gesture toward the bunk. He held the knife up in front of the younger Taggert's sweat-streaked face and added, "I'm going to use the point of this to get his teeth out. And if I hear one more little peep out of you, I'll use the blade to cut your worthless throat. Understand?"

The bristly-haired Taggert was speechless with fright. Angered, Gene put the point of the knife against his nose and forced his head back against the wall behind him. "I asked you a question," he said through clenched teeth.

"I won't . . . won't say nothin' more," he managed.

Old Man Taggert watched in morbid silence as Gene walked back and climbed over him onto the bunk. "Open up," Gene demanded.

Taggert thrashed like a man on fire, but he was using all his strength and getting nowhere for his efforts. His breath was coming in coarse rasps now, and his eyes were wild and unseeing. Gene pulled his pistol and raised it like he wanted to knock Taggert out, but he put it back in his holster instead, wanting Taggert to be fully conscious and able to feel the pain.

Finding it impossible to get into Taggert's mouth, Gene reached into his pocket and pulled out the .50 Sharps shell he had been carrying. "This ought to keep your mouth open so I can work," he said.

He had a firm grip on Taggert's face, but the outlaw twisted and struggled so fiercely that he couldn't get the shell into his mouth. There was a good chance of getting his fingers badly bitten, and so Gene set about using a more tactful approach. When Taggert had settled down some, Gene turned toward the door and called out, "Bull!"

Taggert responded as Gene had hoped he would. The name of his huge son registered, and he tilted his head up in anticipation of seeing him in the doorway. As his head came up to look, Gene gave him a hard rap with the handle of the knife square on the bridge of the nose.

Taggert jerked with the blow and let out a groan as a trickle of blood left one nostril and beaded on the top of his upper lip. His eyes glazed a bit and began to water as Gene forced the shell into his mouth. In an instant, Gene had jammed the bottom of the cartridge into the cavity between Taggert's tongue and lower teeth and had placed the top of it just in back of his upper teeth, leaving it lodged lengthwise in the front of his mouth.

Taggert's eyes widened, and he tried to yell but couldn't. His mouth was propped open so wide, it almost dislocated the jaws at their hinges. He made guttural sounds in his helplessness as the sharp rim of the shell pushed itself into the gums and tissue behind his upper teeth and the base of the shell crushed the fleshy lining under his tongue. He couldn't open his mouth any wider, and he didn't dare bite down or the rim of the shell would push through the roof of his mouth.

Scott turned away for an instant while Taggert moaned. Gene got up from the bed and stood juggling the knife, thinking. Taggert was helpless, and his moans were beginning to turn into a low whine. His bristly-haired son opened up on his wailing again and wouldn't stop even when Gene started over to him. He was throwing his head around like a wild man and blubbering about not wanting to die. It was both sickening and infuriating. Gene pulled his .44 and cocked it. The wailing continued, and Gene put the pistol away and cursed. Then he slammed his boot into the bristly head, and the wailing stopped just as Starky appeared in the doorway.

"We've got to get out of here right now," he said, his face anxious. "That blond kid is back, and it looks like he's got Stringer's bunch with him."

"Where's Janet?" Gene asked.

"She's rounding up horses. I've got to get back and help her. I thought you'd have these two tied up on those horses outside and ready to go by now."

"I changed my mind," Gene said. "They won't leave this cabin alive." He cocked his pistol and aimed it at Taggert's head.

"Damn it, Gene, put that gun down!"

"What have I got to lose? You know I'm the White Bandit."

"I know you're Gene Huntley. I've had a suspicion about you ever since I saw you tracking me that first day on Tongue River. But unless you cause me to think different, you're still Gene Huntley, and the White Bandit is still out in the hills somewhere."

Gene stood silent, his pistol still at Taggert's head.

"It's your decision," said Starky. "I've got to help Janet. That blond Taggert will lead that bunch of thieves up here, and we'll all be sitting ducks." He hurried out the door.

Gene watched him leave and turned to Scott. "I suppose you're on his side, too."

Scott shrugged. "I was just thinking about Janet and how she's changed since she met you. I was thinking how much happier she seems to be. And all because of you."

Gene took a deep breath and holstered his pistol. "Help me get them on the horses," he told Scott.

Gene and Scott pushed Old Man Taggert and his son up onto the horses. Gene had taken the shell out of Taggert's mouth, but Taggert was silent. His eyes were glowing coals, and Scott knew he would do anything he could to escape.

As Gene started to tie them into the saddles, a rush of horses came past them from the flats. Starky and Janet were there with the herd. There was no time to tie the two outlaws to their saddles now. That would have to come later. For now they would have to hope that the outlaws could stay in the saddle with their hands tied behind them.

Scott climbed on his buckskin and turned to help

drive the herd. As Gene swung up on his own horse, the two Taggerts yelled and kicked their horses out into the rush of horses.

Gene cursed and jumped down from his horse, Winchester in hand. He leveled the rifle on Old Man Taggert but had to pull up. The horse herd was running between himself and the fleeing Taggerts, through his line of fire.

"Let's go, let's go," Starky was yelling. "Forget them!"

Janet pulled her horse alongside Scott's buckskin and yelled, "What happened?"

"They got away," Scott yelled back. "I'm afraid before this is over, we'll wish Gene had killed them."

Chapter 18

They took the horses south, hoping they could find a quick way out to the Yellowstone River. Going west would be shorter, but it would mean a slow crossing through the roughest part of the badlands. It was their only choice; taking a stand against the outlaws would be suicide.

Starky hung just behind the herd, stopping regularly to use his spyglass on the trail behind them. The blond Taggert coming from the wood yard with Stringer's bunch had probably found his father and bristly-haired brother by now, and they would soon be coming. Old Man Taggert would stop at nothing now. After what Gene had done to him, and then learning of Bull and LaFarge's fate at the wood yard, he would no doubt want the score settled in blood.

Going out of those badlands on a dead run proved to be the roughest trip of Scott's young life. It was a nightmare of ups and downs and constantly being jolted. The herd was hard to keep together, for they wanted to string out in a long line, and that would have meant losing many of them.

When the breaks finally fell off into a big open drainage with a good flow of water, Scott slid from his

buckskin and flopped on his back in the cool grass. His
breath came in heavy gasps, and he hoped he would
never have to cover some five to six miles through
country like that again.

They had come down into Sand Creek, Scott knew,
for they had reached this country after finding the dead
horses a few days earlier. It seemed like a year now,
and the worst part was just beginning.

Scott got up and saw Gene and Janet leading their
horses toward him. They were looking back, high on
one of the hills behind them, to where Starky sat
glassing the country behind them.

"Damn, I wish he'd just get down here," Gene said
impatiently. He pointed far out to a cloud of dust in the
badlands. "Taggert's after us now. Anybody can see
that."

"We should have a straight run from here down to
the Yellowstone," said Janet. "It shouldn't be that far.
And then we'll be safe."

"Don't be so sure," Gene said. "They'll chase us
clean into Glendive if they have to."

At the creek, Starky had taken his horse down the
hill and was coming across the flat on a dead run. He
pulled his horse up and jumped down. He said nothing,
but his eyes could be read easily.

"Is Stringer with them?" Gene asked.

"No," said Starky. "But I counted ten of his best
men riding with Old Man Taggert and his two sons."

"How far back?"

"It doesn't matter," said Starky. "We haven't got a
prayer."

It wasn't hard to see the outlaws now, riding high
among the hills. Taggert was leading the bunch off the
top into a steep coulee that would come out a short way
down the creek. No matter how fast they pushed the

horses now, Taggert and the rest of his killers would catch up to them. The advantage of knowing those badlands so well had paid off for him. He had led his bunch over a shortcut that he knew would come out about halfway down Sand Creek in hopes of catching them on the bottom. He had figured his timing pretty well. Compared to what lay ahead, the fight at the Powder River was beginning to look like a child's game. Scott could envision all their lives ending here at the edge of what the Sioux had long ago so aptly named Makoshika—the bad land of evil.

Gene took a deep breath and looked up into the badlands where the dust cloud was growing larger and coming closer.

"What do you think now, Mr. Lawman?" he said to Starky with an edge to his voice. "Maybe we can take them all back to stand trial."

Starky narrowed his eyes. "That's not fair, Gene. I try to do my job the best way I know how. I'm a lawman, sworn to uphold a set of rules. I do what I have to do."

"It doesn't always work out, though, does it?"

"Whether it works or not, I have to do it that way. I'm not a strangler or even a regulator."

"Yes, I see your point," Gene told Starky. "But all of us here know there's only one way out of this thing now. And it don't follow the code of the law."

"Maybe so," Starky came back, "but that don't mean the law should be thrown out just any old time it seems easy."

"I won't argue that," said Gene. "And after today you'll see no more of the regulator nobody knows. But right now the White Bandit must ride one more time."

Gene took the cloth mask from his saddlebag and put it on. He looked eerie as he climbed on his horse with only two dark holes for eyes. He pulled a big .50 Sharps rifle from a scabbard on his saddle. He had taken it from Old Man Taggert at the hideout in Makoshika.

"Someone is going to have to keep them off our backs until we reach the Yellowstone with the horses," he said. "It might as well be the White Bandit."

Janet moved over to his horse. "Gene, you can't stop all those men alone. That's crazy!"

"I won't stop them," Gene said. "I'll just slow them down and maybe turn them back until we get a good head start." He pointed out to the long coulee that Taggert and his men had dropped into. "They'll be coming out there before long. It would cost them a lot of time if someone bushwhacked them at the mouth of the draw. A couple of good rifles could do it."

Scott heard the words "a couple of good rifles" and saw Gene looking down at him.

"I'll go with you," Scott said without hesitation. He quickly jumped on his buckskin and took the Winchester Gene handed him.

"We'll catch up with you," Gene told Janet and Starky. "This shouldn't take long."

"Scott," Janet pleaded. "Gene, don't do it!"

"We have to," said Gene. "We have to or they'll be down here on top of us."

Starky and Janet pushed the horses down Sand Creek toward the Yellowstone while Scott followed Gene across the flat to the head of the draw, where they would meet Taggert and his band of thieves.

Scott's heart pounded wildly as he tied his horse next to Gene's and followed him up the hill to where they would make their stand. It was well hidden and a perfect spot for an ambush. The only way out of the coulee to the bottom was past them through a narrow, deeply cut gorge that lay below nearly vertical slopes of solid gumbo and scabby sagebrush. There was no way for the thieves to go around them unless they backtracked to the top and took the next coulee over. When Scott took a position next to him, Gene just smiled a little and said, "We'll see how Taggert likes his own medicine."

In a matter of moments, their targets appeared. Old Man Taggert himself was leading his remaining two sons—the young blond and the bristly-haired one— along with Stringer's bunch in single file over the rough face of the coulee bottom. The going was extremely rough, and they couldn't move their horses any faster than a slow, deliberate walk. So intent were they on watching the trail that none of them gave any thought to the hills above them. Even if they had, Gene and Scott had hidden themselves well, and there was little chance that they would have been seen. Taggert was making himself an easy target.

Slowly and deliberately, the thieves made their way through the bottom and into Scott and Gene's sights. As Scott counted their numbers, he thought to himself how thirteen was always considered an unlucky number.

By the time the thieves knew what was happening, two of their number had fallen, never to get up again. And Old Man Taggert would have been dead himself if his horse hadn't stepped into a hole just as Gene fired the Sharps.

Taggert spun his horse around, cursing in a fit of rage that carried all the way up and down the coulee over the sounds of the rifles. Knowing that the sides were too steep to try to climb and that they would only be better targets if they got off their horses, he led them all in a fast retreat back up the bottom. Scott and

Gene's attack had been well planned. They had waited until Old Man Taggert had led the column almost directly under the spot where they were positioned before they had opened fire. That way the thieves were well within rifle range for quite a while before they could get organized and back to cover. Meanwhile, Scott and Gene took full advantage of it.

Three more thieves, including the bristly-haired Taggert, fell to Scott and Gene's rifles before the band of outlaws reached safety. Gene was deadly with the big Sharps, taking careful and deliberate aim before touching off. The result was always a sickening thud of the slug against flesh and bone that left a hole big enough to put a two-bit piece into where it went in and a gaping hole big enough for a man's fist where it came out. Only one of the victims wasn't blessed with instant death, and it was only a matter of a few moments until that particular thief, whose shoulder had been nearly blown off, bled to death in a pile at the bottom of the draw.

Scott accounted for two himself, including Old Man Taggert's bristly-haired son, who lost what brains he had when he stopped his horse in confusion and looked up toward Scott, who promptly put a bullet just above his left eyebrow. The other victim was one of the bunch Jack Stringer had sent down for Taggert's horses. He was going to put up a fight right there and stepped down from his horse into a round from Scott's rifle that entered just under his arm and scattered his lungs all over his insides.

Scott and Gene both took a few long shots as Old Man Taggert led the rest of the thieves pell-mell back up from where they had come, but none of them scored. Gene cursed as he took one last long shot at Taggert, who was now leading his thieves around the crest of a small hill and out of sight.

"I wish I could have nailed Taggert," he said. "It would have made things a whole lot easier."

"We cut the odds down a lot, though," said Scott.

"Not enough to suit me. If Taggert's horse hadn't slipped, we'd be home free."

Scott looked far up the coulee, through the scattered stands of pine and cedar, to the jagged rock bluff where Taggert had taken his men. "What do you think he'll do now?" he asked Gene.

"Probably climb out of that hole across on the other side where we can't see him and then come down another draw at us farther along the way."

"We've got a real good jump on him now," Scott said. "It shouldn't make any difference now what he does, should it?"

"He knows his way around here real well," said Gene. "He'll have a trick or two up his sleeve, you can bet on that." He turned to look down Sand Creek, his face showing concern. "We've got to catch up with Starky and Janet as soon as we can," he said. "But I would sure like to know what Taggert plans to do now."

"Look," said Scott, pointing far up the coulee. "Isn't that Taggert and his men going up over the top?"

Gene took the spyglass he had borrowed from Starky and studied the far end of the coulee. "It sure is," he told Scott. "Now why would he want us to know which way he's headed?"

Scott spoke up, saying, "I only count six. Where are the other two?"

"What?"

"There were thirteen total to begin with," Scott explained. "I remember counting them and thinking it was an unlucky number for them. We killed three. There should be eight come out of that draw up there."

"That's it," said Gene. "Taggert is sending two down that far draw to try and sneak up on us from behind." He turned to Scott. "You aren't a bad hand to have on my side."

Scott followed Gene down to the bottom of the draw to their horses.

"We'll just wait on the other side of this draw," said Gene. "We should catch them coming around the bottom almost any time now."

Precious minutes passed like hours, time that should have been spent catching up to Starky and Janet. But there was no choice but to wait. There were two of Taggert's men somewhere nearby, and they would have to be dealt with sooner or later.

Finally they heard the sound of horses' hooves on the hard ground near the bottom of the draw. Then two riders appeared below them, traveling cautiously, alert for what they might find.

The two riders dismounted and took position among a group of rocks below. One of them took a spyglass from his saddlebag and settled down to search the country.

"Those two are smarter than I'd hoped they'd be," said Gene. "They'll see us and our horses up here in no time." He leveled the Sharps on their position. All that could be seen were their two heads and the sun glinting off the spyglass. "There's not much to shoot at, but there's no other choice."

The blast from the Sharps echoed up the canyon, and Scott saw rock chips fly just in front of the spyglass. Gene cursed and slammed another shell into the block. "It's going to get harder now."

Both men were on their horses now. One seemed to be holding his face with one hand while he tried to ride with the other. Scott thought he might have rock chips and possibly glass fragments in his face and eyes. The other rider crouched low on his horse and set out fast across the flats below.

While the injured rider tried to get his bearings and set his horse with the other rider, Gene fired again. Scott could hear the scream come clear up to where they sat, and he saw the rider tumble sideways off the horse and jerk for a moment before lying still.

Gene took a deep breath and leveled again on the rider going across the flats. He had a fast horse, and Gene was going to have to shoot quickly before he reached cover on the other side of the creek.

Gene's shot kicked up dust just in front of the horse. In a quick reaction, the horse spooked to one side, throwing the rider off in a tumble of arms and legs. The horse ran free while the rider lay still on the ground.

Gene and Scott rode their horses down to the bottom and over to the fallen rider. Gene got off and turned him over. His head lay at an awkward angle, and one leg was spread sideways. He would never get up again.

Gene climbed back on his horse and turned to Scott. "We've got some catching up to do," he said. "Let's hope we beat Taggert to them."

Chapter 19

Scott and Gene pushed their horses down the Sand Creek bottom as fast as they would go, looking to the hills all the while for a sign of Taggert and his men. It was only a matter of time until six men led by a hate-crazed leader came down another draw onto the flat. Taggert would be more cautious now, Scott knew, but he would be even more determined. The loss of another son and the danger of being killed himself wouldn't stop him at this point; it would only serve to incite his rage even more. Scott had never been around people as cruel and treacherous as these horse thieves. He hoped, if they lived to tell of it, he would never know that kind of person again.

Nearly a week had gone by, with each day bringing about a life or death situation that could have meant the end of their search for horses as well as the end of their lives. They had survived each of those days when the odds against them should have won out. Now everything came down to a matter of minutes, maybe even seconds. Their whole search could end in the loss of everything if one extra second were to turn in Taggert's favor.

Scott breathed heavily while his heart tried to thump

its way out of his chest. It was certain there wasn't much more than a mile left before they reached the mouth of Sand Creek on the Yellowstone. Then, at the same time, he and Gene saw Starky and Janet waving at them with the horse herd just ahead and Taggert leading his men out of a small draw onto the flat just behind them. The time had come.

Scott felt his heart jump into his mouth. The minutes and seconds were still in their favor, as Taggert had at least a quarter of a mile to catch up. But now that Taggert had seen them, it would give the outlaw an extra edge, knowing he had a chance to catch them before they reached the river. Taggert would push his men to the limit. And they didn't have sixty head of horses to slow them down.

Scott waved his hat and yelled at the top of his lungs while his buckskin rushed headlong beside the strung-out herd of wild-eyed horses as he tried to keep them together in one bunch. He could hear the voices of the other three as they did the same thing. They raced at breakneck speed over the stands of mixed brush and grass, moving in and out of the twisted flow of shallow water that was Sand Creek. He waited for the shouts from the others that would tell him that Taggert had caught up to them. The wind was a whoosh across his face, and the ground was a blur beneath him. Taggert was coming! Couldn't his buckskin move any faster? Couldn't any of those horses move any faster? Taggert was coming!

The ground thundered from the pounding of a hundred hooves, and the creek water sprayed in thin sheets as they crashed through the bottom. Birds shrieked from their nests in the tall cottonwoods while rabbits and deer shot out of the brush in panic. Scott's blood was rushing through his head, or was it the roar

of water? Behind someone was yelling something
about Taggert. Taggert was right behind them! And
ahead the rush of the Yellowstone River was an awe-
some sight.

"Scott, Scott!" Gene was yelling. "Scott, turn
them south. It's our only chance."

South took the horses along the edge of the pounding
river, swollen beyond belief from the heavy runoff
flows. The water was a filthy brown that boiled and
raged and pushed its way through and over everything
that stood in its path. They drove the horses the only
place they could, onto a high bank right above the
river.

Gene led them up onto a narrow ledge, and the
horses fell in behind him, squealing and grunting as
they fought to keep their balance on the steep slope that
led up to the trail. He started off at full speed again, and
the horses fell into the pace as Janet and Starky went
ahead of Scott, who was watching Taggert and his
bunch close the gap to a few hundred yards.

The trail skirted the bottom of a giant complex of
hills that rose vertically from the edge of the river for
hundreds of feet, massive walls of shale and loose
rock. Below they could see whole trees and large
pieces of wood and debris being swept along through
the churning water. The sound was deafening, and they
were racing in single file along a thin edge of bank that
hung out over all that angry water. Behind them, the
last of Taggert's bunch was just coming onto the trail.

The trail on the ledge suddenly broke down onto a
small flat area that was just a little pocket that years of
wind and water erosion had carved out of the steep
banks. It was a miniature box canyon surrounded by
steep clay banks and rock outcroppings. The horses
came running down the ledge and, instead of following
Gene's horse across to where the trail started again,

began milling around in the pocket, looking for a way out. Scott joined Starky in pushing them out and got most of them to follow Janet's horse back up the ledge along the river. But there were a few that wouldn't go, a half dozen Circle 6 horses that were wild-eyed with fright and confusion.

"Leave them," Scott yelled to Starky. "Come on! Taggert is right behind us!"

Scott went back onto the trail along the river and started to catch up with Gene and Janet and the rest of the horses, thinking Starky would follow. He didn't. Scott cursed under his breath and was just turning his buckskin around to go back, when the rest of the horses came out of the pocket and onto the trail, with Starky yelling at the top of his lungs right behind them. Behind him, Taggert was leading his men in a frantic rush toward them. He was closing the gap fast.

Scott's blood was ringing in his ears, and he spurred his buckskin forward with a heavy sweat coming down off his brow into his eyes. They had to go faster! The river was pounding and splashing below, and it would swallow them if they went into it. But Scott pushed his buckskin harder. Taggert and his men would show no mercy. Maybe Taggert wouldn't catch them if they could just keep up this pace. Then Scott was gripped with wild fear as his eyes took in a portion of the high ledge they were traveling on farther along the trail.

The ledge was starting to curve in to follow where the river made a big bend. Scott could see Janet across from him, leading the herd of horses along the narrow trail. About twenty yards in front of her was a big washout that cut down the steep hillside, leaving a gaping hole in the trail that was nearly ten feet across. Janet had seen it, but there was no way she could stop her horse without causing a massive pileup of the other horses behind her and sending them all down into the river. If her horse, Clipper, made it across, the chances were good that the other horses would follow in stride. At the speed they were all going, if they didn't clear it, there was little chance any of them would survive.

Janet urged her big palomino to as much speed as he could achieve along the treacherous ledge. He sailed over the washout with ease, not even slowing as he hit the other side. The other horses followed suit, the long line of them making a graceful arc as each jumped in turn. Any other time it would have been a magnificent sight and one worthy of a shout for joy. But Scott's terrible fear was still with him, and his worry switched to Starky and himself now, for he knew how his buckskin hated to jump.

It was too late for worry and too late for him to do anything more than yell and spur his horse on as they approached the washout. In that moment, Scott's fear was reality. The buckskin balked in midstride, just in front of the deep cut, and the horses directly behind crashed into the back of them, startling his buckskin into a frantic leap that nearly jolted Scott out of the saddle as they sailed over the washout. The buckskin very nearly didn't make it over, and Scott held on with both hands and dug his knees in as the horse struggled for footing as the edge of the washout crumbled under their weight. The buckskin regained its balance and lurched ahead into full stride. Scott held his panic-stricken horse up, fearing the worst had happened to Starky.

In the pileup, two of the horses had tumbled over the edge into the river. Starky's horse had come to a jarring stop and had bolted sideways into the bank to avoid the collision, sending Starky off the side into the trail and nearly over the edge himself. After the first two horses had fallen, the rest leaped over the washout in turn while Starky struggled to keep from going into the river, pulling himself back up onto the trail with his arms while his legs dangled over the edge. Once back on the trail, he found himself looking at his own horse as it jumped the washout last, leaving him stranded.

Scott could only continue on to avoid another pileup with the horses that were coming behind him. He cursed himself and screamed aloud. Taggert and his men were just crossing the open area, and they would be upon Starky in less than a minute.

There didn't seem to be any hope for Starky now, and Scott's eyes filled with tears. But new hope came as he looked down the trail in front of him.

Just ahead, the ledge along the river fell off into open country again. Scott's spirits soared as he came off the trail into a bottom where a small stream flowed into the river. The horses had all stopped and were strung out along its banks, gulping water while their sides heaved to take in badly needed air.

Gene and Janet were nearby, their rifles ready for use. As they watched the horses behind Scott join the others at the creek, Gene shouted, "Where's Starky?" and pointed to the empty saddle that hung at a tilted angle on one horse's back.

Scott had already wheeled his buckskin back around and yelled, "He's on the other side of that washout," as he motioned for them to follow.

They raced back to the washout and found Starky trying desperately to climb the hill above the trail. Taggert was just rounding the bend with his men and was only a matter of seconds away. Starky let out a big yell of relief and began to wave his hat in excitement. Taggert arrived and held his men up when he saw three rifles pointed down at them from the slope above the trail. He and his men scrambled off their horses as a volley of rifle fire doubled one over at the middle. The thieves took cover by staying in tight against the steep bank while the wounded one tried to follow and took a heavy spray of bullets that sent him staggering over the edge into the river.

Some of the thieves took potshots at Starky, but they couldn't take careful aim without exposing themselves. Still, each round fell dangerously close, and Starky lay as flat as he could against the hill while bullets thudded into the shale bank beside him.

It wasn't long until Taggert saw how useless his position was and ordered his bunch back along the bank to their horses. Soon they had retreated around the hill and down into the little pocket, out of sight.

"You can't stay here for me," Starky yelled across the washout to them. "Get the hell out of here with those horses and just throw me a rifle!"

"We're not going anywhere without you," Scott shouted back. "We're going to get you up out of there. The only thing that we're going to throw you is a rope!"

Gene and Janet kept their rifles ready in case Taggert should return. Scott took a heavy rope from his saddle and worked one end into a series of half hitches through the bow and around the saddle horn with all the speed he could muster. Satisfied that his end was tied securely, he tossed the loop across the washout to Starky and watched him tighten it around his chest and under his arms.

"You've got no business hanging back for me," Starky was shouting over the rush of the water. "Taggert will be back here in just a shake, and he's got too many men to stand off with just two rifles."

"You just hold on to that rope," Scott shouted back. "We'll worry about the rest."

Chapter 20

"You're all crazy," Starky was yelling. "You've got the horses. You're all safe on the other side of this washout. Why don't you get the hell out of here?"

"I said hold on to that rope," Scott shouted.

"I see you don't have any faith in our shooting," Janet put in.

"See if we ever help rescue you again," Gene added jokingly.

Starky grunted a laugh and prepared himself for what he was about to go through. He was going to have to jump off his side of the washout down about twelve feet into the bottom and let Scott and the buckskin pull him over the top to their side. It wouldn't be that hard, just so he didn't hurt himself in the jump, as the sides and bottom of the cut were brick-hard.

Scott put his horse to work as soon as Starky was ready. Like any good cow pony, the buckskin began backing up until the rope was tight, holding ground and keeping firm tension on the rope as if there was some range cow or squirming calf in the noose.

Starky took a deep breath and yelled, "Here goes," as he moved up to the edge of the cut to jump.

Scott's eyes widened, and he pointed under Starky's

feet. "Look out," he screamed. "Move back!"

Starky's concentration on the jump he was about to make and the loud rush of the river kept him from hearing the warning the first time. Scott kept yelling, and Starky looked down at his feet to see that a big chunk of the bank was tumbling out from under him.

As the bank gave way, Starky tumbled headlong off the edge toward the river. The rope broke his fall, and he let out a loud groan as he slammed into the bank on the opposite side. Scott's well-trained buckskin stood solid against the pull of the rope, and Starky's fall ended with him dangling just above the surging water.

Gene and Janet rushed down the slope and began to help Scott pull him over the bank. They had to keep their eyes focused on Starky as they worked, for the moving water beneath him had a dizzying effect that could easily result in a loss of balance. There was also the danger that the bank they were on would give way in much the same fashion as it had with Starky. All along the trail, the ledge had been deeply undercut by the swirling action of the water, and it seemed almost a miracle that the whole thing hadn't already buckled under the weight of all the horses they had just taken over it.

Starky was about two-thirds up the bank when Gene pointed out some activity farther back on the trail. Old Man Taggert had taken the bunch back along the trail on the other side of the pocket and was lining them all up in single file, leaving a short distance between the riders. Taggert's only remaining son—the young blond—was in front as his father positioned Stringer's men evenly behind him.

They struggled to pull Starky up over the bank, watching Taggert take a position at the end of the line at the same time. What in the world was he up to now? He was beyond crazy at this point; he had become permanently insane and would spare no effort to get his revenge. Old Man Taggert's hand went up into the air, and he waved them all forward like he was ordering a cavalry charge. The thieves moved out along the trail with their horses at full speed.

Taggert was leading his men in a charge across the washout! He had left the distance between each rider so that there would be plenty of room for the horses to jump. His being at the end could only mean that he wanted to be sure that he would get a chance to make it across the washout in case something should happen to the others and that there would be little chance of his not getting in on the kill. Some of those in front might be shot in the first volley, but he would not, and it would enable him to shoot. He wanted to kill; he wanted revenge.

"We've got to get back to that creek," Gene was yelling. "It's our only chance to find cover!"

The sweat poured off Gene and Scott as they pulled at the rope. Janet's eyes were defiant as she held her rifle ready to meet the thieves. Starky strained and groaned and grasped at the bank to help pull himself up. Taggert and his men were just coming out of the pocket onto the trail. Scott and Gene pulled. Starky climbed. Taggert and his men surged ahead.

"Janet, take off," Gene yelled. "We'll catch you!"

"I'm staying! You may need me."

"Janet, take off!"

"I'm staying!"

Taggert and his men kept drawing closer.

"Pull," Gene yelled. "Pull!"

Starky gasped for air as he came over the bank and onto the ledge.

"Let's get out of here," Gene yelled.

Scott's blood thundered in his temples as Gene pushed Starky up on the buckskin behind him. Then Gene and Janet were on their own horses right behind him. Just ahead was cover, a slope dense with cedars that would give them a place to shoot from. Below was the river, pounding and surging and splashing. Behind them were Taggert and his men, only moments behind them.

Scott jumped into the cover of the cedars with Gene and Janet. They would have a better than average chance from there. Taggert and his men would come past and lose at least three of their number before they had a chance to take cover and return the fire.

Scott jacked a bullet into the barrel of his Winchester and got ready to fire. There was a good view of the trail along the ledge as it came off the bottom, much the same as he and Gene's position had been back at the mouth of the draw where they had bushwhacked Taggert and his men.

Then Scott saw Starky get onto his buckskin. What was he doing? Maybe he was going to get his Spencer from his own horse, which was now grazing with the others along the creek. He was going to have to hurry. The blond Taggert had just jumped his horse across the washout, and the others were following.

But Starky wasn't headed for his own horse and his Spencer. He was headed back up the trail toward the Taggerts.

"Starky," Gene stood up and yelled. "Starky, get back here!"

Starky disappeared around the first bend. One by one the thieves jumped their horses across the washout. Scott looked for Starky. The seconds were precious now. Starky still had not appeared.

The last of the thieves, Old Man Taggert himself,

took his horse over the washout and raised a clenched fist in the air. Now it would be less than a minute before the shooting began, less than a minute before it would be decided who would live and who would die. Starky would not make it. Taggert was too close.

Just then Starky appeared, pushing Scott's buckskin as fast as he could. But a shot from one of Taggert's men sent the buckskin into a sprawling skid, and Starky flew off into the grass.

"I'm going down after him," Janet yelled, and rushed to her big palomino.

"You'll never make it back," Gene screamed.

"We've got to block the trail," Scott yelled to Gene. "We've got to keep those outlaws from coming off the trail down onto the flats."

The two of them rushed down the hill and began to scramble up the slope above where the trail broke off into the meadow. Taggert's blond son, the first rider, saw them and crouched low in his saddle. He and the others were shooting at Janet as she rode out into the open to try to help Starky. The shots from their rushing horses were going wild, but it would be only seconds before they hit the meadow.

Scott and Gene fought to keep their balance on the slope above the trail. Bullets hit near them as they tried to maintain a steady position on the slippery clay bank and aim at the same time. Then, as the blond Taggert went through the little pocket where Starky had been, his horse turned a complete somersault and rolled off the bank into the river.

The young Taggert had been crushed in the fall, and he lay in a crumpled pile in the middle of the trail.

The rider behind jerked back hard on his horse's reins. The horse squealed in pain and rose high on its back legs, fighting the steel bit that was tearing into its mouth. Gene set off the Sharps, and the round tore a ragged hole in the rider's throat. One of the thieves behind crashed into the rearing horse and knocked loose a large rock from the hillside.

In the same instant, a large portion of the badly undercut bank gave way under the weight of the rearing horse, and the two riders went off into the river with their horses and the big chunks of earth that had split apart from the hillside. Almost immediately, other portions of the bank began to buckle. More thieves went over the edge, screaming and waving their arms in wild panic as the rush of foaming water sucked them down. Most of the horses would be strong enough to swim to shore, but none of the men would; they were all swept away with only an occasional hand or leg sticking above the brown current. There was one small section of bank that remained, and Old Man Taggert was trapped on it.

His horse had thrown him in the confusion and had gone over the edge with the others. Now Taggert was the sole survivor on an isolated piece of ledge that was already starting to crumble.

Scott and the others couldn't have saved him if they had wanted to; he was too far away. They could only watch as he tried desperately to climb the steep shale bank above him, sliding back down each time and finding less and less bank left for support.

Gene raised the Sharps and leveled it on Taggert. He looked down the barrel for a long moment and then lowered the gun. Finally the bank cracked away completely and the old man tumbled into the churning Yellowstone River.

Starky was up on his feet and Janet was helping him over to where Scott and Gene stood watching as Taggert disappeared under the current.

"He's gone now," Gene said to no one in particular. "They're all gone." He took the big Sharps by the barrel and heaved it into the river. "They're all gone," he repeated. "It's all over."

"I just about got us all killed, didn't I?" Starky said, breathing hoarsely and holding his side. "I owe the three of you my life."

"Are you hurt bad?" Gene asked. "You took quite a jolt when you fell off that bank. And that last throw from Scott's horse couldn't have helped."

Scott had the buckskin and was rubbing its neck. It had only stumbled and had not been shot by one of Taggert's men, as he had feared earlier.

"I think we owe you as much as you owe us," Scott said with a twinkle in his eye. "I think I know why that blond Taggert who was leading the bunch went down in that tumble with his horse. You said you carried that fishing line along to catch the big ones. Well, you really got a big one that time."

Starky smiled. "It was a good thing those two cedars were across from one another on the trail like that. It made for something to tie to."

"What?" said Gene. "You mean the reason you pulled that fool stunt of riding back up the trail was to string up fishing line?"

"I thought we needed an edge," Starky said with a wink.

"You show me where that's written in the law books," Gene said jokingly.

"It must be in there somewhere," Starky said.

"If you say it is, then it is," Gene said. "I'll get to reading in those books as soon as the roundup is finished. It'll do me some good." He took his white mask and gave it a fling over the bank into the river. As it washed down and out of sight into the current, he repeated, "It's all over. The White Bandit lives no more."

They all walked down the bank to the little stream, breathing easy for the first time in nearly a week. The horses were rested now and switching flies in the shade of the cottonwoods along the creek. It was a good feeling to have time to settle back and relax for a change.

They ate their midday meal on the west bank of the Powder River. The water had gone down considerably from the first time they had forded, and they pushed the horses back across with no trouble. Everyone was loud and joyous; it was time for celebration.

Finally Starky announced that he was going to leave for Great Falls. It was a long ride, and he needed to get back. As he got set to leave, he said to Janet, "Do I get a kiss from the bride to be now, or do I get an invitation to the wedding?"

Janet blushed. "Starky, how did you know? We haven't said anything to anybody."

Starky grinned. "An old lawman has his ways."

Janet leaned over and gave him a soft kiss on the cheek. Then she gave him a firm hug. "Starky, you've been so good to me. I'll never forget you."

"Now, now," he said to her. "The world ain't so big that folks can't see one another on occasion." Then he took Gene's hand and squeezed it firmly. "You're a damn good man, Gene. I wish you and Janet every happiness."

Finally he turned to Scott. "Young feller, you've proved yourself a man this week, just as much a man as any I have ever known. You make something out of that Circle 6 outfit you've got now, you hear?"

He climbed into the saddle and turned his horse north across the hills, giving them a long wave before he eased his horse into a gentle lope that took him out of sight.

The rest of the day would take them over into the Tongue River country, Scott knew, and the following morning would find them on the Rosebud. Under the stars that night, Scott knew that he would think of Starky and the happiness Gene and Janet were now sharing and the past that was behind them all. He would think of the pride and joy he was going to see in his pa's eyes when they crested the hill in the early light with the Circle 6 horses and many from the neighboring outfits. As Scott watched a hawk ride the wind high above them, he thought to himself that there would be a lot of good days ahead.